TBB

Dedicated to

Danny, Conner, Chris, Kani, Becca, and Deirdre.

For being more than friends.

For being family.

Contents

RED LIGHT

Driving late at night was never something I enjoyed. There were too many variables that could go wrong. A headlight could go out, I could get lost, maybe even fall asleep at the wheel, and worst of all break down with no one else awake to help fix the car. But I had work in a few hours, and I'd already taken off as much time as I could. Dealing with sick parents wasn't easy, especially when you had to help pay medical bills.

With the radio playing softly, I spared a glance back at Sam who lay sleeping in the back seat, his white tipped ears relaxed against the side of his head while his paws twitched as if someone were tickling his feet, but he was too tired to wake up.

Turning my attention back to the road, I groaned as we approached a stoplight. Why they had these sprinkled through the long empty expanse of highway I didn't know. It wasn't like anyone else was going to be awake at two in the morning. If they were, they were likely just as irritated about stopping as I was. All I wanted was to be home. To get a little bit of sleep before dragging myself out of bed for work.

Easing down on the break, we crawled to a stop. The front end of the car kissing a long white line that you weren't *supposed* to cross. Sighing, I relaxed against my seat and took a moment to close my eyes. This was a mistake. Every part of me wanted to curl up and fall asleep on the back seat right next to Sam. He'd be warm and more than happy to share. He'd most likely spare me a few kisses to the cheek for good measure before using me as a pillow.

Muttering a curse, I forced my eyes open to find that the light was still red and impossibly bright. Its vibrant red glow reflected across the dark road creating a radius of light that far surpassed normal stoplights while intensifying with each second. Part of me knew it was impossible to have a streetlight that bright. There were regulations to follow for the safety of drivers, but there it was. Like an angler fish luring unsuspecting prey. Glowing intently in a realm of darkness.

"Change already," I grumbled, running out of patience. There was nothing worse than having to sit and wait for an unreasonably long light. "I can't believe this, Sam."

Startling Sam awake as I uttered his name, he poked his head out between the driver and passenger seat, ears swiveling about on high alert. I got the impression that he could hear the hum of the strange red light. That the electricity within was so intense it fried the wires encased in black metal.

Still, the light didn't change. My impatience turned into anger and against my better judgment I placed my truck in park before opening the driver side door. Sam made a move to leap into my now empty seat when I stopped him.

"Stay. I'm just having a look, okay buddy? Something must be broken." Giving Sam a pat on the head, I rolled the window down so he could still see me before shutting the door. He hated it when I was out of sight and I hoped this would soothe his nerves.

Sure, part of me knew I could just run the red light, but I had the worst luck a person could have. A cop would inevitably fall out of the sky to ticket me should I attempt such a mildly illegal action in the middle of nowhere.

Running a hand through my hair, I scanned the side of the road for an electrical box. Maybe someone had hit it and rather than reporting the incident drove off, leaving everything inside slightly askew. Only, from what I could tell, there was no electrical box. Rolling my eyes, I turned back to the cross section of the road.

Walking out into the middle of it I glanced left and right thinking that maybe an electrical box was on one of the other adjoining roads. Tucking my hands in my pockets, I fished around for my phone in hopes that the flashlight would illuminate something I missed.

Fingers brushing against the device, I pulled it from my pocket when a gust of wind ran its ice-cold fingers down my spine. It startled me enough to drop my phone. It landed face down in the road, the flashlight miraculously turning on to blind me with red light. No, that wasn't right. How could it be red?

Blinking furiously, I bent down to collect my phone when another gust of wind swept through the intersection. Along with it came the smell of thick stifling oxygen. I didn't realize there was a dense coating of fog drifting across the road until my phone's red light danced through the suffocating cloud.

"Great. Now there's fog. How the hell am I supposed to drive in this?" Returning my phone to my pocket, I turned curtly on my heel. If anything I could get back in the truck and wait for the fog to clear out. It never lasted more than a half hour from my experience, but as I turned around, I found myself face to face with more fog. The truck was nowhere to be found.

At first, I figured I was too tired to remember my journey away from the truck. I had to have turned about in the wrong direction; but after completing a full circle my heart started hammering in my chest. I couldn't see a thing beyond a few inches in front of me.

"Sam?" My voice rang out in panic. One that he would have easily heard, and as if on cue, he barked in reply. "Good boy Sam! Keep barking!"

He offered up a few more calls much to my relief. Listening intently, I did my best to walk towards them. One foot in front of the other was easy enough until even my feet disappeared in the fog. Swallowing tightly, I tried not to panic more but the entire situation was so unreal I felt like I was hallucinating.

No matter how many steps I took and no matter how much Sam barked, I didn't seem to be getting any closer to him.

Stifling a panicked yell, I closed my eyes like I had before. That's when all of this started. Maybe I had fallen asleep after all. Maybe I was dreaming. But when I opened my eyes, I was met with a set of lifeless ones in return.

A gaunt pale looking fellow stood before me. Their eyes were cloudy and white. Blind. Their hair thin and wispy, their skin translucent and yellow.

"What the fuck?" Scrambling back a few steps, I tried to create as much space between myself and the stranger. That's when my eyes settled on their feet. Fragments of what used to be shoes stuck to their ankles and toes with fresh and dried blood. Their skin was blistered, raw, and shredded. Their left foot much worse than their right with sections of bone exposed on the ends of their toes. "Oh my god. Sir. Are-you need help."

The words barely left my mouth before, yet another gust of wind sent a new plume of fog to sweep the man away. To my left I heard sobbing. With intense worry, I turned towards the noise. The cause of it was a young woman stumbling about and shielding her eyes while bare feet left a trail of blood in her wake.

"Ma'am?" Again, the fog came. It swept her away like it had the man, and it was then that I realized it was sweeping me away too. All the while the red streetlight grew brighter and brighter until it became unbearable. Were these people lost? Was I lost too? Would I become something like them?

Heaving in desperate breaths of air, I struggled to come up with some sort of logical conclusion to this mess. There had to be a cause to what I was seeing, but when a third person miraculously appeared in front of me I ran. I didn't know what else to do. I needed to find my truck and leave as quickly as possible.

"Sam! Sam!" My voice tore from my throat sounding harsh and ragged. There was no response this time. I was alone. Now, with tears streaming down my face I wandered around, arms extended and hands grasping. All I wanted was to touch the familiar metal frame of my truck and lock myself inside.

Shivering from head to toe with a thick layer of sweat coating my skin, I pressed on. There was no telling how long I walked for. Whether it was hours or days but all that drove me was desperation and rage. Rage to get out of this suffocating red light. It bounced off the fog bombarding my eyes from every angle. It became so intense, so bad, that my retinas began to ache. That's when I closed my eyes, promising never to open them. That didn't work. The light was so intense it burned clear through the backs of my eyelids and into my brain. Searing any sense of sanity I had left.

I was stuck in the middle of nowhere, wandering, weak, tired, and blind. I would die here inevitably. Still, my legs moved until they couldn't anymore, and I was left in a crumpled heap upon what I assumed was the road. Fog devoured me like a flesh hungry beast and part of me wanted it to win. To consume me and put me out of my misery.

It must have sensed my desire because a wet slobbery tongue raced across my cheek. Hot breath danced along my face and I knew I was a goner. It had finally beaten me into submission. That stupid red light had won.

Then a soft gentle bark resonated in my dying ears and the greatest sense of relief I'd ever felt washed over me. "Sam."

I'm not sure what happened next. All I know is that I regained some form of consciousness in a blurry white room where incessant beeping bombarded my senses. I could barely make out a set of wires dancing along my arms when a door eased open and in walked someone decorated with a lab coat.

"Ah, you're awake. How are the eyes?" They asked, their voice gentle but prying.

"I can barely see," I rasped, my throat feeling like it was full of razor blades.

"I see. Well, we can get an optometrist in here shortly- "

I didn't let her finish.

"What happened?" I demanded, aware of the doctor setting a blanket across my mid-section. I had a vague sensation of coldness racing along my toes.

"Officers found you miles away from your car clear into the next county. You were missing your shoes," the doctor explained, pausing as if debating whether they should tell me more. Truthfully, I didn't remember losing my shoes. "Your feet were shredded. You'll need skin grafts in the coming days to help them heal. Your dog is the one who led the police to you. When they found you they said you were rambling about a red light."

As the last two words of her sentence registered, my heart sank into my stomach and everything from the previous night came rushing back to me. All I could see was the bright red light searing into my eyes. I couldn't look away no matter how hard I tried. We stared at each other even as a plume of fog rolled in to consume me. Smother me. Kill me one mile after the other as I walked aimlessly in red colored silence. It was here, with me in this hospital room. I could feel it. The same impending dread and doom along with the growing pain in my eyes. It wasn't going to leave me alone. Not now, not ever.

"Sir. Calm down. You're safe." The doctor's voice was muffled in my ears. Mixed in with the sound of quickening beeps. She called out for help; her voice filled with the panic and fear I felt. People rushed around me, poking me, prodding me, but all I could see was that light. Bloody and red like my feet.

Of course, the doctors and police got talking with one another after that. They said I had some sort of psychotic break the night of the drive and its effects carried over into my hospital stay. That the stress of my parents had triggered something in me. That being tired and driving hadn't helped. That something deep within me snapped. They wanted a psych evaluation to help me, but it didn't matter. Ever since the doctor said those fateful words all I could see was red.

It never left. Never faded. Not until I made it. They told me they couldn't save my eyes. That was fine. I didn't want to see that damned red light anymore. But no matter how many times I told my story no one believed me. Not the doctors or the psychologists or anyone. I know what I saw. I lived it and I have the scars to prove it.

Maybe you'll believe me or maybe you won't. Just listen to me when I tell you this. Don't drive in the early hours of the morning. Don't waste your time at a red light like I did. Run it. Run it fast and don't look back. A ticket is less of a pain than gouging out your own eyes. And if you do stop at the red light and it stares back at you a little too long with a little too much intensity. Don't get out of your car.

An angler fish knows when it's captured its prey. Knows how to keep it locked behind a set of teeth unable to leave without help. Knows how to devour you slowly. Those red lights? They're traps. And if you aren't careful the fog will find you. Just like it found me.

Chimney Weepers

When I was little, I used to hear the chimney cry. It never scared me; it just made me sad. Nervous even. I'd heard stories of young chimney sweepers getting stuck in those tall brick columns just trying to do their jobs. It always worried me that some poor little boy was stuck up there alone to suffocate in ash, but no matter how much crying I heard from the soot-stained structure, my father told me not to look. He was adamant that investigating the noise was useless.

He chalked the muffled sobs up to the wind. That the breeze from outside was blowing over the chimney top like one did an empty bottle only instead of a soft whistle it was a soft cry. When I got old enough to question his explanation about the wind, he told me it was just the sound of the house groaning. I'd heard of houses moaning and groaning before. It had something to do with the old architecture of buildings. I guess it wasn't so different than old people moaning and groaning either.

For a little while I chose to believe my father's explanation but on particularly stormy days the crying grew worse and it was hard to ignore but then again, maybe dad was right. Maybe the house was just groaning. If I got rained on and knocked around by wind the way my house did, I'd be vocal about it too. So, despite my doubts I assumed my father was telling the truth.

It wasn't until I turned eleven that I stopped believing the house was groaning. By now, father was fed up with my questions about the crying. At this point he was grasping at straws for explanations. If it wasn't the wind or groaning house, what would make the chimney sound like it held a crying little boy within its brick confines? As far as I was concerned, he couldn't talk his way out of it this time.

"The chimney is crying again," I remarked, staring at the shuddering structure as lightning arched in my peripheral. Outside a storm was raging like it never had before. The newspapers had discussed flooding and Father bought sandbags to place along the doors. If it kept pouring like this sandbags alone wouldn't do much to prevent rising water from seeping into the house.

"I told you, it's the wind," Father sighed, smoothing out the napkin in his lap. He was always dropping food on his pants.

"You know I don't believe that," I countered, eyes drawn to the chimney yet again as its sobs carried on.

"The wind makes the house groan and the noise echoes in the chimney," father carried on, chewing agitatedly at his dinner.

"You know I don't believe that either."

A careful silence settled between the two of us. Outside, thunder tumbled against the dark sky as if some ancient God were laughing at our disagreement. I supposed to some sort of primordial being, a conversation like this would seem pretty funny.

"What will it take for you to stop worrying about the damn chimney?" Father frowned, his hands settling on the table. His index finger drummed nervously along with his heartbeat.

"I don't know," I admitted. "I'd like a reasonable explanation at least. Something plausible."

"Fine," father nodded, pursing his lips. "Long before you were born, when the house was just being made, a little nine-year-old boy was cleaning the chimney. He was one of the only ones small enough to fit inside of it. Or so they thought. He got stuck. That night a storm came and drowned out his cries. He sobbed and yelled for help, but no one heard him over the thunder and rain. His body was found days later when a stench began to fill the house. The chimney has cried ever since. It hasn't been silent for decades."

"So, it's a ghost then?" I asked, trying to fathom the fact that I supposedly lived in a house with a haunted chimney and that this was considered a plausible explanation.

"No." Father's voice was stern, and his eyes had grown hard in the dim light. Another clap of lightning followed by a bellow of thunder accentuated his remark. "It's worse than a ghost. That's all I'll say."

"Are you just trying to scare me?" I asked, a smile tugging at my lips.

"Yes," father nodded, leaning back in his seat. "The only ones who mess with the chimney are the sweepers. That's the rule. You remember that don't you?"

"Of course! You always said, 'it's too dangerous to mess with and if you get stuck trying to climb inside, I'll laugh at you before I help.'" While the rule never made much sense to me, I suppose he really was worried I'd try to make my way up the chimney and somehow get stuck. After all, I had a way of getting into places I shouldn't. I'd been that way since I could crawl. It terrified mother back when she was alive.

Taking father's word at face value I tried not to dwell on the crying chimney any longer. Maybe it was just haunted. If I was a nine-year-old chimney sweeper who'd gotten stuck and died, I'd also haunt the house responsible for my untimely death. In fact, I'd probably do more than just cry all the time. I'd do my best to annoy anyone who lived in the damn place.

Without too much concern regarding the matter I moved on with my life and grew used to the noise. Its usual drawl was just as persistent as the sound of an alarm clock. Annoying but not horrible. It wasn't until a month later that things changed. The crying worsened. It was so loud and so horrible I couldn't sleep.

It bellowed out of the chimney like a wailing toddler, crawling up the stairs to sit right outside my bedroom door. What was worse, the crying sounded real this time. As if someone were in trouble. It occurred to me then, that just yesterday the chimney sweepers had come by, and a pit began to settle in my stomach.

Had another little boy around my age fallen in and gotten stuck? Was the chimney cursed? Did it just so happen to swallow children whole? Heart hammering, I clambered out of bed determined to see for myself who was in trouble; if anyone. Running down the hallway, I didn't even try to be discrete as my bare feet slapped against the floor. The closer I got to the chimney the louder and more desperate the wails became.

"It's okay, I'm coming!" I called, slowing to a stop beside the fireplace. Catching my breath, I leaned forward peering up into the hollow dark. The crying continued for a moment more as I tried to decipher some sort of body in the dark. "Can you hear me? It's going to be okay!"

As my voice carried out, I expected it to echo through the hollow space before bouncing back down. If there was a boy stuck up there, he'd hear my distorted words. Only, my voice didn't echo. It didn't move at all. Something had stuffed the chimney full. So full my words were shot back at me in an instant. Silence persisted as the wailing ceased.

Frowning, I hesitantly stepped forward into the fireplace and peered directly up into the darkness. Something was wrong. The chimney had never stopped weeping before. Swallowing tightly, my stomach coiled in a sense of dread. I'd made a terrible mistake. As sweat began to bead along my brow, the darkness began to move, contorting and shifting

17

with the sound of chiton scraping against brick. Whatever I was looking at was unnatural.

Frozen in fear, all I could hear was a mocking cry from the moving creature as dozens of twisted spider legs crept out of the chimney to clutch at the frame of the fireplace. Then the big deep dark shifted and a pale face stared back.

It belonged to that of a young boy, nine years old, but where his eyes should have been there were none. Instead, the skin of his eyelids had fused with the skin of his face and the bulb of his nose had been worn away into snake-like slits. A mouth like that of a saddened mime twisted across his pale face in the expression of a distressed and silent cry.

The head was mounted on a strangely long neck, like that of a praying mantis. Frozen in place, my vision grew dotted as I struggled to breathe. The creature, whatever it was, leaned down with its long arching neck and paused so that our faces nearly touched. From within the contorted mouth, a set of dripping mandibles emerged, pushing taught skin aside so that it stretched painfully thin. With a sucking noise, the mandibles settled into place, a slobbering gooey ooze decorating the pointed ends.

It was then that I screamed but no noise came out.

Stumbling back from within the fireplace, I scrambled towards the hallway. While I retreated in fear the creature tumbled from the chimney with a heavy thud as its body hit the floor. Its spider legs scratched against the ground attempting to seek purchase but gaining none as its great dark mass wobbled from side to side. It wasn't until a set of humanoid hands protruded from the centipede shaped torso that it steadied. With a shudder, ash and soot tumbled from the monster's body as if it were made of the substance. Tilting its head, the creature's mandibles began to click in some type of amused chatter. It was then that I snapped out of my wide-eyed stare. Watching the creature with the fear of a child who had seen the devil and did not run, I half crawled half ran back to my bedroom.

Closing the door and locking it I dove beneath my bed aware of the scraping outside my door. As spider legs tickled the floor in an eerie sort of manner, tip-tapping like the impatient drumming of fingers, I held my breath. The beast, whatever it was, lingered outside of my bedroom door, fumbling with the handle. At some point it attempted to throw its weight against the frame. A violent shudder seemed to shake the entire room as I prayed for safety. Thankfully, my bedroom door held fast.

Trembling from head to toe like a frightened dog, I dared to peer out from beneath the confines of my bed. It was then that the creature tried and failed to loosen the lock. It was smart, too smart for something that grotesque. In truth, my only saving grace was that the monster couldn't see. Otherwise, it would have spotted the key set atop a small table beside my door. Beside it was a picture of my late mother.

With an impatient groan, muffled sob, and the frustrated stamp of spider legs, the beast retreated. Despite this, I didn't feel safe. Unable to sleep that night, I lay awake very much aware of the silence now permeating through my house. There was no more crying. No more weeping. The absence of sound alone was unnerving. Clutching a worn stuffed dog to my chest, I buried my face against its soft hide seeking some semblance of comfort in the dark.

For a moment I found peace until the sound of insect legs scuttling over the roof interrupted my tranquility. A strange sort of thud sounded outside as the beast's disgustingly large body hit the ground. Lingering beneath the safety of my bed, I foolishly left it behind to peer out the window.

What I saw would haunt my dreams for the rest of my life. There, out on the street was the creature in its full glory. Its spider legs shone in the moonlight, its centipede body shivering and writhing while tiny legs that couldn't reach the ground moved in thin air. The white face frozen in a silent sob stared intently at a stray dog whose bark was sharp and loud. The poor pup, as brave as it was, didn't stand a chance. Two scrawny pale arms embedded amongst the entanglement of insect legs scooped the scraggly dog up as mandibles chattered excitedly. I looked away before I could witness the poor creature's demise, but the bitter sound of a pained whine echoed in my ears.

Sick to the stomach, I retreated to my bed and buried myself beneath the covers as if it would protect me. From that night on I was never the same.

In the following years, I documented what I could of these creatures, hoping to save my children from the fate I'd endured. When they were old enough, I revealed the truth and now I reveal the truth to you.

Chimney Weepers are a strange type of monster. They aren't exactly a ghost or a demon, they're far too real to be any of that. They're the culmination of death stained in soot, suffocated by ash, drowned by storm, and left to die within the suffocating confines of brick. Whoever and whatever dies within those chimney walls emerge anew in a terrifying fused glory. It's because of this that I came to believe in God and the Devil. Only they would be responsible for a reality where the Devil has abandoned them, and God has abandoned us.

Bloodbath

The first time I saw her I was alone. The water in the bathtub had just been turned off by my mother. She tested its heat to make sure I wouldn't be burned before setting me in the white basin. A singular rubber duck floated along tiny waves as I positioned myself at the back of the tub to lean against the rim. Having just reached three years of age, I was old enough to not need constant supervision but that didn't keep my mother from sitting on the toilet and reading a magazine just in case something went wrong.

Despite the emptiness of the tub, my imagination compensated for the lonely rubber duck. It was stuck in turbulent waters desperately trying to find its child amidst a horrendous storm. Whether or not it succeeded was up to me.

Splashing about in warm water, I occupied myself with the senseless adventure until I grew bored and began to properly wash myself. Syrup from that morning's breakfast had somehow gone unnoticed and stuck painfully to my left elbow. Scrubbing harshly at the spot, I smeared away the remnants of syrup and left behind pink tender skin.

At first, my attention was too wrapped up in cleaning myself to notice the way the water darkened. It was clear, but somehow it contained a shadow that hadn't been there before. Then came the ink. It swirled about as if being spilled, originating from the stopped-up drain, and oozing between the crease of the stopper and the tub.

It coiled about like a series of snakes until a long white hand reached for my chubby leg. Innocently, I placed the rubber duck in the hand and retreated further against the rim of the tub. The hand groped along the duck as if searching for something until letting the yellow creature bob off on a new adventure.

A second hand appeared, weaving through the water until it settled on the metal stopper. I watched both in curiosity and uncertainty as long fingers plucked the stopper up. The moment the rubber released, and the water began to stir, two glowing black eyes shone back at me from within the drain. They remained unmoving and unwavering. Slowly, they blinked, and a strange eyelid slid across their swollen pupils.

I couldn't help but recoil. Something wasn't right.

My developing uneasiness grew when those two strange hands began to claw their way towards me and out of the drain came a wispy looking woman. Her lips were impossibly thin, and her skin was translucent in such a way that I could see the blueness of her veins amongst the inky water.

She drew closer to me. A smile contorting those paper-thin lips until suddenly the drain gave a drowning cry and my mother snapped shut her magazine. My eyes refused to break contact with the strange woman who was slowly being sucked back down the drain along with the last remnants of water.

At last, my mother collected me from the bathtub and wrapped me snuggly in a warm fluffy towel. Even as we left the cursed room, I stared intently at the empty tub expecting the woman to crawl up from the drain once more. The door shut smoothly behind my mother, and whoever was living in that drain temporarily disappeared.

For some time, I grew used to the woman's presence when she appeared in the tub. She wasn't a friend per se, but she hadn't done anything to harm me. Not at first anyways. Instead, she helped me in my games, often moving my little rubber duck about in the tub while I grappled with other toys. My uncoordinated self-had a tendency to lose track of what I was holding, and she carefully returned the missing object to me.

Quite frankly, I liked her. She kept me company when I was little and lonely. To me, she was the closest thing I had to a friend at that age and for a while everything was peaceful. We existed simultaneously without incident until my eighth birthday.

That evening after my party I struggled to remove temporary tattoos (due to my mother's insistence) when the familiar woman re-emerged. She blinked slowly from within the drain but there was a lack of recognition in her twisted features. Her dark black eyebrows furrowed in unison with her narrowing eyes. Once more a sense of uneasiness settled over me.

I watched frozen not in fear but surprise. She had always made sure to stay away. There was a mutual understanding that we wouldn't touch one another but here she was reaching out towards me. Her long spindly fingers white in color with prominent knuckles and sharp jagged nails cupped the flesh of my calf. Breath hitching in my throat, I waited anxiously for something to happen.

My eyes remained locked on hers and for the life of me I couldn't look away. Not when the water ran red and her nails bit viciously into my leg. Only when she blinked could I avert my gaze. It was then that I saw the meat of my leg exposed. It didn't hurt, not at first, but I knew now that something had changed in our relationship. This woman was not my friend.

Frightened, I lunged for the drain and drew up the stopper. Heart pounding, I didn't wait until the water drained before stumbling out of the tub. Blood continued to roll down my leg and all I could do was cry for help. My mother, bless her soul, raced into the bathroom to help. Her eyes widened in fear as she glanced between me and the bloodstained bathtub.

That night I was taken to the hospital and no matter how many times I explained what happened, the doctors didn't believe me. My own mother told me I was talking nonsense. That I didn't want to get in trouble for screwing around so I'd lied, but I could tell by her eyes she didn't believe what she was saying. There was nothing to explain my injuries other than what I'd said and I knew my mother was a superstitious woman. She believed me, she just wouldn't admit it.

For a while after the incident, I refused to bathe with anything other than the hose in the backyard. There was no reason to risk further injury as far as I was concerned. The scar on my leg was enough of a warning for me. I wasn't welcome in the bathroom and certainly not the bathtub.

This went on for a few years until my mother insisted, I was too old to be standing naked in the backyard washing off with a hose. In truth, my fears hadn't left me, I just feared my mother's wrath more. From there on out, I showered quickly with just enough soap to keep from stinking the next day. It wasn't until I left for college that a sigh of relief escaped me. I was free.

With time, I began to forget about the woman living in the drain. Papers and coursework were enough to occupy my mind and rid me of old memories. It was nice while it lasted.

Fifteen years passed without another incident until my mother passed away in a car accident. At first, I wanted nothing to do with the house until I learned that it was left to me. Up until that point in my life I planned on staying as far away from my childhood home and its bathroom as possible. Only, the love I had for my mother outweighed my childhood fears. She always said I had an intricate imagination. I suppose part of me believed her and I tricked myself into thinking I'd made up the specter woman that used to haunt me.

The first week I spent in the house was a lonely and quiet one. I slept in my mother's bed, comforted by her scent and feeling that somehow, she was watching over me. All the while I avoided my portion of the home. There was no reason for me to brave the dark hallway leading to the bathroom.

At night I lay awake thinking back on how many times I'd seen the woman lurking in the drain. Part of me wondered if I was going mad. Maybe there was something wrong with me. Perhaps I needed a doctor or some sort of medication.

I did my best not to dwell on the past for too long, but I was only human. Eventually it became all I could think of as if her presence were consuming me, and I knew I had to take a stand. I'd spent most of my life being terrified of that stupid bathtub. I wasn't going to let myself die fearing something that I likely made up as a child.

Swallowing tightly, I slipped out of bed and padded across the house down the long dark hallway to the bathroom. Easing open the door, I regarded the tub with great distaste. Reluctantly, I shed my clothes and turned on the faucet. The water came to life and spurt from the pipe with vigor, tumbling into the tub eagerly. As water pooled in the white basin, I placed myself at the back of the tub, so my back settled against the rim. Tucking my knees to my chest I waited, watching the drain intently.

Reaching out, I hesitantly turned the water off before settling back in my old position.

There were times I held my breath in anticipation before my vision grew fuzzy and I was forced to recollect myself. Slowly, the water grew cold, and I feared that I had gone insane. I was convincing myself of meeting a specter that didn't exist. Shivering, goosebumps decorated my skin, and as I reached to undo the drain a ghostly hand settled upon my own. Breath hitching, I turned the water on again as if that would flush away the wispy hand. It didn't.

Instead, the spectral woman took shape, appearing exactly as I remembered her. Dark hair draping loosely in front of her face with dark eyes peering out from behind it. Her naked frame was frail with translucent skin pulled taut across sharp angled bones. For a moment she sat in the same position I did, knees tucked to her chest, arms wrapped snuggly about her frame, and head lowered in uncertainty.

Licking my lips, I briefly glanced at the door, having left it open in case an escape was needed. When I returned my gaze to the woman, she was in front of me, close this time, leaning in with her cold breath dancing across my cheeks. That strange clear eyelid flicked across her eyes as a trembling hand cupped my chin to tilt my face up towards her.

Again, I found it hard to breathe, and just like when I was little, I realized I couldn't look away even as the water began to spill over. It spattered the floor in clear sheets, sweeping up against the wooden cabinets beneath the sink.

A single long black nail trailed across my jaw as deep dark eyes studied my face. There was a sense of familiarity in the woman's gaze that I couldn't quite place. For a moment I was comfortable, and I noticed a certain kind of sadness settle in her eyes. Her bottom lip jutted out ever so slightly and I feared that I had wrongfully upset her.

Her lips parted albeit parched and cracked. Her teeth were impossibly white as her hand trailed down to my neck.

"You aren't my baby anymore," she whispered, tears welling in her eyes. A pain flared in my chest at the sadness I'd inevitably invoked. I recalled the way she once played with me and the way she turned against me on my eighth birthday. I'd grown too old for her I suppose. Looking back on it, I began to understand all that had happened. She had lost someone; I was sure of it.

With a sigh, I settled my hand over hers, some instinctual part of me understanding what was to come. "You aren't going to let me go, are you?"

Warmth fell over my fingers and ran down my wrist before pooling on my shoulder. I didn't have to look to know what it was or what she had done. I'd felt the sensation of her claws before.

Alone and cold, the only company I had was her. The presence of some spectral woman coddling my fading body. She was strangely warm, and a bit of life seemed to return to her as my head fell against her chest. Part of me understood that I wasn't the first person she had held like this before. The way her nails bit into my skin indicated her fear of losing me. I noticed a look of severe regret etched into her features. Not at what she had done, but because she had loved me.

Now, it was like she'd grown disgusted with me for having grown up. For having abandoned her when I didn't have a choice. Despite this, she remained by my side humming a strange sort of lullaby as the house I grew up in flooded with blood-stained water.

The rise and fall of her chest nearly lulled me to sleep. Clinging to the last bit of consciousness I had left, I peered through bleary eyes watching as she stared at the drain with some form of longing. Then, with careful precision, she plucked up the stopper of the tub.

Red swirled together like a tornado slowly being swallowed whole. As a child I used to watch her vanish, retreat to where she had come from (wherever that was) and wonder what life was like for her. Now, I wasn't so sure I wanted to know. As if sensing my distress, the woman whispered some form of reassurance as a shuddering breath left my lungs, and I too washed down the drain.

Puddle Jumpers

Children have a natural curiosity about them. One that often leads to trouble whether good or bad. It is their desire to learn, observe, and experience that fuels them from a very young age. So much so that drops of liquid tumbling out of the sky is amazing enough to warrant an adventure. An adventure that induces such excitement they lose all forms of proper judgment.

It is in these situations that impulse gets the best of them. Nevertheless, as crystal puddles pool on the ground anticipation bubbles in a youthful chest. Puddle jumping is something akin to basic instinct. It is a desire found in the very bones of all youth that I knew of.

Swallowing tightly, I glance left and right as if crossing the road before approaching the puddle. Someone is already there laughing, giggling, and stomping about in red rubber boots. Red was a color one grew to love with time and exposure. Colors don't mean anything unless associated with something worth caring for, but red is a color that I had come to adore. In fact, I was a bit jealous of how vibrant those red boots were. I'd never seen something so fresh and bright up close before. It was only ever from afar that I could view brilliant reds. My mother said it was better that way. I suppose she was right because the color stirred something awful deep within my chest.

Curious, I realized that the other child hadn't noticed my arrival. Instead, they continued to make a mess of the puddle sending droplets into the sky with ones that were already falling down. There were no parents in sight. While it may have been strange to some, it wasn't too strange to see children out and about on a rainy day exploring all it had to offer.

Pausing, I observed the other child with care. Rosy cheeks only brightened with exertion as each jump took a spurt of energy. Tiny teeth were white and unstained. Those teeth were bright like red boots. Red and white went well together.

Thunder raged above breaking my concentration with a violent start. With another crack of lightning the other child became alarmed. I watched as their bottom lip trembled. When children cry it is never a good thing. In the wild a child's cry is dangerous. It gets them killed more often than not. Predators find it to be charming. Sort of like music.

Only, I had never heard a child's unbridled cry of fear before. The way small lungs sucked in sharp breaths of air to produce siren like noises was almost terrifying. How could something so small make such a loud ruckus? Surely, *I* hadn't made such noises. If I had, I most likely would have been scolded or shunned. It was good to be quiet and unnoticed. Otherwise, people would catch on.

The more the sky fought with itself, the louder the child cried. It's small wails turned into louder ones before devolving into yells of a primal nature. It was no longer as horrifying as it once was. In fact, it was beginning to feel normal. Natural. With a shiver, I stood waiting; expecting a mother to swoop in and collect her offspring. Mine would have, but no one came.

The crying continued, shaking the child's slender frame. I couldn't help but notice that those red boots did little to help in such a terrifying situation. Frankly, I would like to take those red boots. Besides, no one was there to stop me from taking them, were they? Focusing on shiny red, I forgot about the horrendous crying.

Why was red such a pleasant sight?

A flash of white teeth drew my attention yet again as a wide-open mouth garbled out another cry.

Slowly, the other child's body wracking sobs fell in line with the thunder creating a strange sort of music. One that filled the chest and radiated outwards with force. Tilting my head, I watched intently. I couldn't help but shift focus between red and white as the music continued to grow. Was the sky playing along or the child? At this point, it was hard to tell but that didn't matter. Time ticked by slowly, and every ounce of movement in my body seemed to cease. A tight swallow later and everything came rushing back.

At last, the song crescendoed and a violent shriek radiated into rolling clouds. All that existed was red and white and screaming until it became one gigantic mess. For a moment the world stilled along with the rain and its puddles.

Red swirled about in a vibrant paint as splintered white mixed within it. Red boots floated, suspended in the puddle for only a moment before being placed on my small, webbed feet. Red was such a nice color. While I wasn't exactly sure what had happened, I found that I wasn't ashamed to have silenced the screaming child. After all, that's what Puddle Jumpers did.

Smiling to myself, I regarded the bloodstained water above. As the sky began to clear and the sun re-emerged, it looked like a beautiful mosaic. I'd never been good at painting before. How pretty. Pushing aside a faceless slender frame, I examined the paths before me. Where should I go? Should I go home and tell mother what had happened? Would she be pleased with me? Was I not a young hunter to be proud of?

A glance down at red boots solidified my answer as a new set of laughter echoed in the distance. Laughter was nearly as good as screaming. Smiling, I regarded the glittering portals above. Head cocked to the side; I listened intently before determining which puddle I ought to take. Then I jumped and along with me came red boots.

Wallpaper Flies

Flies are a strange sort of thing. Often, they exist as single entities zipping about quaint homes creating an annoying buzz. Other times they flit about picnics in the park looking for scraps to fill their microscopic bellies. It is a dreary and meaningless existence. One dependent on temporary survival.

Then there is a mass of pulsing, twitching, and vibrating creatures which smother the walls of a poorly wallpapered bathroom. The mass' voice is ominous. A warning to passerby that the room is taken. Occupied. Meant to be undisturbed. Little legs grace soupy water in search of sustenance only to be sucked in by a pudding-like texture. For a moment, tiny ripples emanate from the sacrifice. Then a quivering sludgy mess stills all at once no longer lapping lazily at soaking bones or sloughing skin. As the water stills so does the vibrating mass as if some unspoken agreement was uttered between bathtub and wall. In time the trembling black fuzz lets out a collective sigh. There is a joint identity now. One that does not understand the circumstances of its surrounding environment, but one that realizes becoming a million flies is far more exhausting than dying.

They do not remain undiscovered though. When the stench becomes suffocating, strange men in well pressed suits crowd into the molding bathroom with notebooks containing scribbled notes only a doctor could read. They acknowledge the flies with contempt,

"You know James," sighs the tall balding man as his partner opens a window that was previously smothered by dying black specks, "I hope I never die like this."

His partner regards the gaunt mangled form of the deceased perched awkwardly in the bathtub. Bones decorated in paper thin sagging skin sit at awkward angles as the muscles which once held them in place are consumed by death's hands. Chapped lips lay taught against yellowed teeth and the flesh of the nose is no more. Even more haunting are the set of hollow eyes staring vacantly at the fly covered wall. The wall stares back. Nothing is said as James struggles with the idea that inevitably, everyone becomes a squirming bulge of flies looking for escape. Like them we are specks in a universe *entirely* too big. One mass collectively existing. Nothing more. Nothing less.

"James?" A hand settles on his shoulder reminding him of his duty.

"Sorry." Taking a step outside, James collects his thoughts with shallow breaths. The balding man remains stuck in a molding bathroom with peeling wallpaper and a rotting stench. He contemplates. Then he regards the buzzing black mass as his companion had. How does one kill a fly and more importantly how does one kill a million of them?

"I'm surprised no one called this in sooner," the bald man coughs, using his shirt to cover his nose.

"Who are they?" James asks, eyes drawn back to the buzzing squealing mess.

"Mr. Crowley. Retired fireman," his partner explains, wiping beads of sweat from his brow. His complexion has paled drastically. James doesn't blame him.

"Crowley," James repeats, licking parched sweat-stained lips. The wall shudders excitedly for a moment at the sound of a name they had no right to recognize. Eyes falling to the ground, James notices the humidity stains on the baseboards decorated with growing mold.

"Come on James, take some pictures of the gentleman for our report," the bald man insists, his head now glistening with sweat that races down the back of his neck in thick trails. Stifling another horrendous cough, he steps outside leaving James alone.

"Alright, hold still," James sighs, hoisting up the camera dangling around his neck. "Just a few pictures, Mr. Crowley."

The flash ricochets across the room a dozen times before James leaves the building behind. He returns to the station with his partner, camera in hand and a buzzing in his mind. The pictures are sent away as soon as they arrive, and James wastes away in his office mind running wild with the images of deceased Mr. Crowley. The day stretches on slowly but surely until the moon makes its ascent and a clock screams that it's time for the young officer to go home.

With a cigarette tucked between his lips, James wanders down the streets until he crosses paths with the building. Eyes traveling up to the fourth floor, he mentally reconstructs the interior knowing what lay hidden in those old brick walls. Swallowing tightly, he crosses the street, enters the building, and follows the horrid smell to his destination. Easing the door open so as not to disturb the occupants, he ventures into the bathroom.

Like before the smell hits him hard, but this time the buzzing of his mind is accompanied by the buzzing of the wall. In the dark, the quivering mass was almost unnoticeable save for the faint glow of his cigarette. If it weren't for the persistent humming no one would have been the wiser, but James knew. He'd seen Mr. Crowley with his own eyes. He knew where the poor gentleman rested.

Alone in the silence, James' phone startles the dark with a chipper ring. Sighing deeply, the young officer answers, "James here."

"James what in the hell were you thinking with these pictures?" It's his partner, angry and spiteful. "You were supposed to take images of Mr. Crowley."

"I did," James protests, not understanding the callousness of his co-worker. Drawing in a long breath from the cigarette, the tiny flame smolders a little brighter revealing a million little eyes staring back at him.

"No, you didn't." Comes the short reply. Short like his partner's temper. "No one gives a shit about a bunch of flies James!"

"Maybe not," James shrugs, aware of the buzzing becoming far clearer than it had before. He's certain he can hear a million renditions of a singular name reverberating from the wall. "But they aren't flies."

"Of course, they are! What in God's name are you talking abou-!"

Before his partner can finish, James ends the call, setting his phone upon the cracked veneer counter. He takes another long drawl from his cigarette and stoops down to pry open sticky wood cabinets. He rifles through the contents for a moment before collecting a tall skinny can with strange cursive letters. Popping the cap, he moves to stand before the quivering mess and with hollow eyes of his own he regards the ones staring back.

"Would you like to go now?" James asks, the buzzing intensifying as he draws near, the smoke from his cigarette upsetting Mr. Crowley. "Hmm. So be it."

Drawing the cigarette from his mouth, he taps the end of it sending out a shower of sparks while pressing down on the nozzle of the can. A jet of clear spray shoots out catching hold of the sparks and igniting them into proper flames. The big black tumor of Mr. Crowley ignites in an instant, a million little wings burning up all at once as tiny voices cry out in relief.

The young officer stands there as the fire grows ever wider swallowing Mr. Crowley until nothing remains of him but a charred pile. Nodding as if doing a great service, the young officer leaves the burning bathroom behind taking the apartment steps one at a time, his shoes squeaking on metal steps. With a calm breath he draws out another cigarette, opens the door, and takes to the barren street as fire alarms scream in the background. Flames lick out of apartment windows and the sound of wailing sirens echo in the distance.

As he walks, puffing at the deadly roll of paper tucked between his lips all he hears is the sound of a million flies dancing around inside of him. Buzzing as if they wanted out. Setting a hand to his temple he attempts to soften their cries. It doesn't work. With a shiver, he continues down the road, the vibrations persisting. A million flies wanting to be free. A sullen whisper drifts into the dark, ignored by the rest of the world save the moon. "It's not time yet, friends. It's not time."

And as he wanders the darkened pavement, tiny wings litter the ground behind him with each thrum of the heart.

Dead Girls Don't Get A Say

When you told me you loved me, I didn't think you meant it. You always seemed so hesitant to say those three words and when you finally did my heart stopped. I'd waited an entire lifetime just to hear your affections. To feel them the way I felt them. In another world I would have called it a miracle, but we both know it was just time that did it.

I don't think time heals all wounds because it didn't heal mine, but I do believe that time reveals our true nature. With time you learn things about yourself that otherwise lay deep beneath the surface. Experience leads to discovery and discovery experimentation.

If only you'd loved me sooner. Maybe then I wouldn't be so overwhelmed by your feelings.

Feelings that are more intense than I could have imagined. Your love is a passion that burns so fierce and brightly it transcends the physical plane. If God were real, he'd feel it too.

Yes, I know I used to believe in him. In the afterlife. The kind where you'd enjoy a lifetime of bliss without strife. Can you blame me for wanting it to be real? Perhaps it was just a desperate attempt to combat what I already knew. If God really did exist, he was just like you.

Sweet, kind, and all too loving but only after time. Time would always run out. As I watch you, I try to understand your heart, but I can't. Why now do you love me so? Why after all this time do you lavish me with such affection?

Believe me, my heart still yearns for you, but this is never what I wanted. My fantasies about your touch were pleasant. You'd caress my skin with feather light fingers leaving without a trace when you were done. Your lips would ghost across mine and I would feel the heat of your breath on my neck. The simple thought of you holding me so close would send a shiver down my spine.

I still shiver, but it isn't as pleasant as it used to be. There is something in your touch that I can't quite explain. It isn't distant but it isn't familiar. Not like I imagined. Maybe that's my own fault. That I dreamt of this moment so much I was not prepared for the harsh truth that it really was just a dream.

As my breath hitches for the umpteenth time your teeth graze against my neck and I'm reminded of what you truly are. Again, a shiver. You smile at the sensation, enticed by the tremble in my frame not knowing that it wasn't my intent.

Feeling the sputter of my heart I know that time wears on and I am reaching the end of my rope. Once upon a time I would have loved to spend that tiny length of rope with you. To be held like I always wanted. Now I wish more than anything I kept the idea of you a fantasy.

That the feel of your hands did not exist. That you kept the whispered words 'I love you' to yourself. As my throat grows dry, I feel the flutter of my lungs. This is it. It's time. For a moment there's fear, and then it's like falling asleep. Slowly I hear the voice of God vibrate against the shell of my ear as my chest burns but I can't hear what he says. Not as the steady thrum in my ears comes to an end. Still, he speaks. Still, he touches. His teeth have now set in. Time. I wish I had more of it. Maybe then I could escape you and your holy words.

But I can't escape, and I'm reminded of the time you told me that when people die, they can feel everything from head to toe. That you never truly leave your body. I used to laugh at such sentiments. That couldn't be the afterlife, could it? Why would we spend our entire existence conscious on earth only to be conscious in the ground?

Now, as I feel the tug of reality upon my lifeless frame I understand. God really is like the men he creates. He too has set his teeth in me. He has held me tight from the dawn of time so that now, as my heart stills, the man I love can truly love too. This was my destiny. God's plan as they say.

While I grapple with this feeling of betrayal, I succumb to the understanding that no one really loves you when you're alive. Not like this. Not with teeth and skin and tight gripped hands. Not the way it was meant to be. Love in death was always the intention, wasn't it? There was no sacred grave, just temporary storage.

As his claws scratch at my skin, mine scratch at the grave. When he's done, I feel nothing. He feels everything. And then, as if I were dreaming, his lips ghost across mine and I feel his breath upon my neck. If I could weep I would as the love I'd always envisioned is tainted by his touch.

But what could I do? Dead girls don't get a say in how they die after death. Girls don't get a say in anything. Not in the Bible, not on earth, and not in time.

As he leaves, I'm resigned to the fact that so long as there is flesh on my bones I am wanted. And while I have always wanted to be wanted, I can't help but wish he'd wanted me sooner.

Radio Static

As a child I loved listening to the radio. Very rarely did I understand what anyone was talking about, but the second I got my hands on a radio of my own, I had many sleepless nights.

While new radios were too expensive for my family to purchase, my father found the one I came to possess at a thrift store. It'd been donated some time ago by a young gentleman, and now it had found its way into my lap. Riding home with it in the car was the most restless I'd ever been. I wanted to turn it on and waste away listening to sports announcers or politicians campaigning over things I couldn't comprehend.

Getting home took eons until finally my father's rickety old truck rolled into the driveway. It'd barely come to a stop when I slid out of the passenger's seat and raced into the house. Darting into my room, I dove onto my thin mattress and dug around for a set of batteries in the nightstand. After scrounging up a set of double As and plunging them into the radio, my little fingers twisted the radio dials in every direction possible. I waited impatiently for the small box to come to life. After what felt like hours a raspy voice broke through, carrying across my room despite being no louder than a whisper.

At first, I thought it was some sort of sports broadcast, but I quickly discovered that was far from the truth. Instead, the raspy voice began to talk in broken segments as if the receiving signal was bad.

"Your daddy lost his job," the voice choked out. Silence washed over me and for a moment I contemplated talking back. Shaking my head and biting my tongue I disregarded what had been said and continued to fiddle with the dials. The signal never changed. "There's a reason he never buys you anything nice. He's a wash-up and you know it. A high school dropout with no future."

Swallowing tightly, I set the radio on my nightstand and retreated to the corner of my room. How in the world was this thing talking to me? It couldn't have been possible. Then again, that was a radio's job. To talk to people.

"You hate him. You just haven't realized it yet. He spends more with alcohol than he does with you. He cares more about the bottle than you. He loves being poor more than you." The radio rambled on as I did my best to ignore it. I loved my father. He was a hardworking man. Sure, he liked to drink from time to time but he was stressed. I could forgive him for that. It wasn't exactly easy being an only parent in a world like this. All I knew was that from the moment I was born it was the two of us against the world.

Shivering from head to toe, I abandoned my room and sought out my father for comfort. He was sitting slumped over on the couch with a can of Pepsi in his hand and a lukewarm plate of chicken nuggets in his lap. He asked me what I thought of my radio and while I wanted to admit that it terrified me, I didn't want to disappoint him. After all, he'd wasted seven dollars on it. Seven dollars that could've gone to a decent meal. Instead, he'd invested it just to make me happy and feed my interest in radios. Seeming pleased with my answer, Dad switched the tv to college football and together we lounged on the couch for the rest of the night as he explained plays and rule changes to me.

Eventually, I began to nod off and with a warm chuckle dad picked me up in his arms and carried me to my room. Peering through bleary eyes I watched him pause and regard the radio for a moment before settling me into bed and lowering the radio's volume. Yawning, I curled up on my side and closed my eyes.

At some point in the night, the radio's hum became a voice once more. It called out to me through the shroud of my dreams and poked at my slumbering mind. It said things that were cruel. That my father was planning to abandon me. That I was going to be a failure just like him. That I'd somehow end up alone in the world with everything set against me.

In the morning the radio continued but as time passed its claims and lies grew evil. It spoke of a time where even the devil would be proud of me. That I would become someone so strange society would cast me aside until I either killed myself or had someone else do the job for me. By the time I was eighteen I could barely sleep at night. I spent days at school napping in class and failing my courses from sheer exhaustion. It became so bad that they removed me from campus due to 'behavioral issues.' I was too emotional, too lazy, too everything. But the worst part was that I couldn't give them a good reason behind my behaviors. No one would believe me if I told them the truth. So, I took the punches, and I took their punishments.

The day I was kicked out of school I contemplated ending it all then and there. It'd be easier than going home and having to face my father. Despite such temptations, I came clean, and my father promised to love me no matter what. That alone nearly killed me, but what really hurt was how the radio laughed. Its sickening cackle sent waves of shame through me and all I could do was lay in bed crying. That night as I stared at the ceiling through bleary eyes, I was forced to come to terms with the fact that I'd not only failed myself but my father too. And that at the end of the day, the radio was right. I *was* shaping up to be just like him. No one wanted me. No one cared. I was just another failure.

"I knew you'd realize I was right," the radio giggled, a sigh following the outburst.

Biting back anger, I sat up with a pillow in hand and attempted to smother the laughing radio as if I could suffocate the voice inside. It didn't work. I could still hear its disturbing rasp radiating in my skull.

"I told you. You're just like your daddy. Useless. You know it's his fault you ended up like this don't you? He didn't provide for you like other parents do for their kids. Deep down inside, you know none of this would have happened if he'd been a better father." While I wanted to argue with the radio, deny its statements, I couldn't. Despite myself I felt resentment growing towards my father. He *could* have worked harder, drank less, went back to school, and tried for a better life but he didn't. In doing so he'd set me up to fail. He'd created an exact replica of himself and passed his miserable fate onto me.

The next morning, my father tried to comfort me with a homemade breakfast, but I couldn't look him in the eye. All I saw was a reflection of myself. A version I would despise until the day I died. Stifling my feelings of rage, I went about the day angrier than I'd ever been before, and while I want to say that was the last time I ever listened to the radio, I couldn't. Something about it pulled me in.

Over the next few years, I struggled through mediocre jobs until I left home and never looked back. Maybe it was unfair to do, but I hated my father for the life he'd given me. It was because of him that I could barely afford a one-bedroom apartment in the middle of the ghetto. It was because of him I had this stupid radio in the first place.

"You think this will save you?" The radio asked from where it sat on the table as I ate. "You think this little apartment will keep you from becoming your father? From being a failure? From becoming what you're meant to be; a pathetic little man."

"Shut up!" I spat, gripping my fork tightly.

"Give it time. You'll see just like before; you can't run from this. No one can." The radio gave a small coughing fit before going back to its incessant hum. Now agitated I tried to busy myself with other things like reading, playing video games, and more, but nothing worked. All I could think about was what the radio said. I spent days ruminating on its remarks until I drove myself to the bottle. It was the only way I could forget about things. The only time the radio's voice and its hum left me alone.

Eventually, I learned to tune it out. It'd begun to repeat itself and as I continued my day-to-day life it became as boring as everything else I experienced. That was until someone new came into my life. She was beautiful, charming, and intelligent. She didn't hate me for my lousy excuse of a home or pathetic job as a cashier at the local supermarket. She enjoyed my company, listened to me like I was a normal human being, and brought me snacks from the bakery downtown.

It wasn't long until she moved in with me. That was a mistake.

"She's using you," the radio laughed.

"That's not true," I whispered, eyes settling on where she slept.

"It is! You give her a free place to live. She'll save everything up and leave you. Just like your mother left your father. Maybe you'll even get a kid out of it and the cycle will continue." As much as I wanted to disregard the radio, I couldn't. It'd been right one too many times before.

And just like before I found myself growing bitter. I distanced myself as much as possible from her until I couldn't take it anymore and she roped me back in. I loved her too much to give up, but the radio preyed on my love. It weaponized the one good thing I had in my life against me. For the most part I could take it until one day it broke me in a way I couldn't explain.

"She's cheating on you," it declared, a certain smugness to its voice. "Why else is she coming home late every night?"

"She's working," I protested, attempting to focus on making dinner.

"That's what you're supposed to say. You know it's true though. You can't provide for her. You can barely provide for yourself. You've done nothing but become a leech to society. A waste of space even worse than your father. There is nothing you could do to satisfy her. Not in life and not in bed. She's found someone better," the radio insisted.

As the little box continued its prodding my grip on the iron skillet tightened until my knuckles turned white. Wincing as the handle dug into my hand, I tried to focus back on dinner. "You're just a stupid radio. You don't know what you're talking about."

"Of course, I do!" The radio laughed. "You're a tiny man in a world too big. If you know what's good for you, you'll

51

save her from the same fate your father gave you; a poor miserable life spent wallowing in a pit of disappointment and self-pity."

Heart pounding as blood rushed to my ears I turned about to glare at the stupid radio. "If you're so smart then why don't you manage my life for me?"

"I have." The words were cold and callous. I could almost picture the strange man inside offering up a shrug.

As I registered the short admission, something cold settled in my chest as if my lungs filled with ice. "I should've gotten rid of you a long time ago. You're just a radio!"

"And you're just a man," the radio mused as my hand settled back on the skillet. Not caring about its contents, I collected the heated weapon and made my way around the kitchen to the table. "You can't hurt me, you know."

"Yes, I can!" I spat, raising the skillet above my head. "I'm not what you say I am."

"You're right," the radio's voice softened for only a moment, "you're not what I say you are. You're what you tell yourself."

Blinking slowly, I felt something painful twist in my gut. Guilt gripped me followed shortly by anger as the skillet crashed down onto the box with a violent thud. The first swing came easily along with the second, third, and fourth. Suddenly I was bashing the remnants of the radio into the table until it shuddered threatening to give way. All the while the crumbled box started to laugh. No matter how much I hit it, it kept on laughing.

"What are you doing?" A voice rang out behind me near the doorway, but I couldn't stop. Something inside of me had consumed every logical facet of my mind. As long as the radio laughed, I'd continue to destroy it. "Stop! Samuel, stop!"

Arms wrapped around my torso tearing me away from the table as I continued to swing wildly and scream. "This isn't my fault! You did this to me! You did this!"

Shaking from head to toe I toppled onto the floor panting and sweaty all the while aware of a strange warmth covering me. The world above swam in and out of focus as saddened laughter continued to ring in my ears. I lay there trembling, completely oblivious to sirens blaring outside as cops swarmed through the doorway with handcuffs. Rolling onto my side I looked past the unconscious form of my girlfriend who lay bleeding beside a skillet. Crying like an infant, I fought to stay conscious as paramedics raced into the apartment.

As chaos unfolded around the room, radio static accompanied the scene. A radio static that had always been there. A radio static that could only belong to a seven dollar broken radio found at the local thrift store.

All around me a plethora of noise crescendoed until at long last the world began to fall silent. The radio's saddened laughter faded away along with its lingering hum. Relief rushed through me as the room began to tumble in on itself. With spit decorating my lips as a paramedic withdrew a needle from my arm, I glared at the table through bleary eyes. "I win you bastard. I win."

Silence encased me as they carted me off into the night strapped down to a gurney destined for the mental hospital. It was the quietest my life had ever been, but back in the apartment my radio continued to sing its static little tune as a body bag covered the face of my girlfriend and a skillet was collected from a blood-soaked floor. As the apartment became empty the radio remained, destined to find another. Destined to consume you with its radio static.

The Whittler

A small shed tucked behind a slanted sun-worn house harbored a tall wiry man with a beard too big for his face, and fingers twisted from overuse. Sunlight passed between slats in boarded walls and through holes drilled by dutiful woodpeckers resulting in distorted shadows taking shape on a dust covered floor.

The smell of cedar was thick in the air along with a musty scent of sweat and damp wood from last night's rain. Running a hand over a half-shaped image, the man blew away specks of dust as he carved out the crevice of a bear's ear. His sullen gray eyes scanned the creature for defects, criticizing even the smallest misstep in his work. One couldn't capture life itself in a piece of wood if flaws were embedded within it.

Humming a low tune, the Whittler trailed a calloused thumb across the piece of wood before swiftly dragging a knife across its surface. The blade grated smoothly on the material, shedding a thin slip of wood that fluttered lazily to the floor. It landed with a soft sound, padded by the dust upon the ground.

Slowly, humidity grew within the shed as the morning sun dipped lower in the sky. As heat continued to bathe the outside world, mosquitoes made their way inside settling comfortably on weathered old skin. Soon, red pock marks grouped together with old ones as the bugs began to feast. The Whittler didn't flinch.

Instead, he continued to carve away, gradually making progress on his project until at last he had done all that he could. Once more, he inspected the wooden figure. Then, with an agitated huff, he chucked it aside where it landed heavily in a pile of identical figures. The eyes weren't right.

He could never get them right.

By now, the Whittler was impatient. He wanted to try again, but he had sense enough to head back inside his blue painted house and wait until tomorrow. Even still, he lay away at night thinking about the mountain of failures tucked away in his shed. One of these days he would get it right. Perfect, even.

Eventually, morning came with the violent scream of a neighbor's rooster. As much as the Whittler hated that damn bird, it kept him from worrying about an alarm clock, and like every morning he moved from his bed to dress in worn dusty clothes. For breakfast he ate oatmeal, grinding his teeth and ignoring the unflatteringly stale taste. Routine was routine. It ought not be broken.

After a quick stretch, he stepped outside, and took a moment to regard the sun before vanishing from sight. Tucked away once more in his shed he picked up another piece of wood and set to work.

The beginning of the process was easy enough. On occasion he held the creature up in the light and turned it over searching for mistakes. Like always, he found one, but he would finish the little bear no matter what. That's what you do despite mistakes. Shuffling his feet beneath the table, he kicked at a set of warped floorboards. The large oak beside his shed was beginning to root above ground and disrupt the shed's foundation.

If he wasn't so old, he'd bother to fix it, but there were better things to do. In time, mosquitoes came, and again he created a dismal failure. This rendition of a beautiful bear met its brothers in the mass grave of wooden figurines.

Clenching his fists, he abandoned the shed with a slam of the door only to continue the process all over again day after day. So much so, that the stool he sat on was beginning to form to his rear. Long ago, there had been a cushion to pad the hard surface. That too had worn away with time.

At some point, the sound of a record player scratching at vinyl took shape. Music carried throughout the shed lilting gently and dropping into somber notes. Kicking aside the mountain of abandoned bears, the Whittler cleaned off a portion of his work bench to place a small cooler. In it lay a series of meals kept cold by a set of ice packs.

Sniffling and running a hand through his beard, the Whittler sat in his usual spot, a strange sort of determination taking root within him. Today was the day. He was going to get the carving right. He'd decided it last night while lying in bed and staring agitatedly at the ceiling.

Swiftly collecting a piece of wood, the Whittler began anew, scratching and chipping away at it with ease. Tapping his foot to the music, he lost himself in the project and environment. Completely unbothered by the harsh light making its way inside, he let his hands do the work and his voice do the singing.

Hours passed and he only stopped for a drink, sipping lightly at a cool bottle of water. The condensation felt nice against his calloused hands, but shavings of wood stuck to the plastic surface dirtying its once pristine exterior.

At some point, darkness fell upon the world outside, cooling the interior of the shed to a bearable temperature. By now, the Whittler had tossed aside his first attempt in frustrated dismay. Frowning so deeply that lines began to etch into his face, he began again, and again, and again.

One after the other until his eyes hurt from staring at microscopic details. Blinking fiercely, he carried on without the help of sunlight. That was fine. He was experienced enough to go by feel. Tracing the outline of the project, he worked until morning when again the harsh sun emerged.

How long this cycle carried on for, he wasn't sure. How many failures had he created in the pursuit of success? Again, he wasn't sure, but that didn't matter. He'd promised to get it right.

Outside, birds began to join in his song singing happily with his raspy voice. It would have been charming if he weren't so focused. What was worse, the damned tree roots beneath his bench finally broke through the floor. When exactly it had happened, he had no clue, but it was a nuisance, nevertheless. He could no longer comfortably tap his feet to the music dancing about the shed.

With shallow breaths, the Whittler remained focused, avoiding all distractions. Anyone who knocked on his door was promptly ignored along with any creature skittering across the roof. All that mattered was his work. Not the sun, not the music, and certainly not anything outside.

As shadows began to move across the floor, he cast aside another bear. Running old aching fingers across the surface of a new piece of wood, he noticed a knot in it and tossed that aside too. Time and time again things were tossed aside until he was fumbling in the dark for a new piece of medium.

Hands skimming over something that seemed the appropriate size he felt his heart still and the clawing form of anxiety left his throat alone. He hadn't run out of wood. He was fine. He could still work. Still get it right. He'd promised her he'd get one right. For a moment, the Whittler paused as the beautiful face of a blond little girl came to mind. She was small, five years old with freckles, two quarter-sized dimples, and a light in her deep brown eyes he could never forget. She'd had an affinity for bears. Something she'd begged him to carve long ago. Something he promised he would, but it had been lost to other projects. When the time came to make it, that silly wooden bear, she was already gone. In the end, he was too.

As the image faded, the Whittler's mouth screwed up tightly in consternation as he found that his tongue was impossibly dry. Almost like sandpaper. How long had it been since he'd had something to drink?

Shaking his head, he waited impatiently for morning to come in hopes of successfully finding another bottle of water somewhere in the desk. In the meantime, he continued to whittle away. Unwavering in his determination, he ran through three more projects.

By now it had to have been morning. He could feel it in his bones, but the birds were no longer singing, and neither was he. The Whittler had fallen silent some time ago, but he could feel his own parched lips moving. He knew the lyrics of his favorite song, but where had it gone off too?

Swallowing tightly, he rubbed his ears in hopes that something would happen. Nothing did. Had the whole world fallen silent? If it had, when did it happen? And where was the sun? Had it run off too? Biting at his lower lip, the Whittler anxiously trailed a hand over the wooden object upon his desk. It was still there. Still present. Again, his anxiety faded along with any apprehension he had for his project. He needed to finish. This one would come out right. Feeling the soft wood upon his finger pads, he carved out the details like always. Sure that he was doing everything perfectly.

The motions became so familiar that with time he could no longer tell the difference between what he was or wasn't doing. Once there was warmth, a strange sort, but that too had gone away and in its wake was a strange sort of numbness. The lack of sensation was more alarming than anything, but he pressed on. He could do this. He could get it right. He would try again.

Again. Again. Again. Again. Again.

Then what?

Well, he would try once more.

That's what it seemed like anyways. For a while he succeeded in carrying on. In persevering, but not all men know the difference between passion, obsession, and madness. If anyone were to wander into his cluttered little shop, they would notice the mountain of wooden bear figurines stacked up to the roof. The ones closest to the bench were stained with blood and more misshapen than their earlier counterparts. Despite the Whittler's certainty, his latest attempts were chiseled by seemingly unskilled hands.

As for the stool he sat upon, it too was ugly. Warping in the center it seemed that the Whittler's dust stained jeans had fused with the surface. Even if that weren't the case, he wouldn't have been able to leave even if he wanted to. By now, the oak tree's roots had taken hold, growing up around his boots, ankles, legs, and torso. It wrapped him up like a cocoon so that only his arms stuck out from the elbow down and his head from the neck up.

Leathery skin lay dehydrated against his face, and his eyes remained open with dilated pupils that had long since forgotten how to adjust to sunlight. He had gone blind in his unblinking frenzy. His hands, which had always been gnarled, were now ruined. Worn away from so much possessive work that only finger bones erupted from stumps of skin. Ears which had once been able to hear were shattered by the constant noise of a blaring record player which somehow still spun in the humid shed, its song carrying on as if there was still work to be done.

Perhaps the worst part of it all resided in shredded vocal cords. Persistent singing while charming at the time, had condemned the craftsman. By the time he realized he needed help, he could no longer ask for it, but no one would have heard him anyways.

In a cruel twist of fate, it seemed that only the oak tree would know what became of the man. Frozen in time, the Whittler's greatest creation would be the preservation of madness; a Whittler who could whittle no more.

Window Runners

It was common for me to imagine creatures running alongside the car late at night. In fact, it was one of the few things that kept me awake for the long drive home. As much as I loved karate practice, spending forty minutes in the car to and from the studio was a bore. Sure, there was the radio and even a podcast or two, but the radio got repetitive, and the podcasts got too predictable.

So, what was I supposed to do other than use my imagination to cook up some strange little creature running 60 miles per hour down a dark road? As far as I was concerned, it was a creative outlet. Something my mother encouraged me to have so she couldn't complain too much about it, could she?

Settling my face against the cool glass I let my eyes scan the wilderness as it flashed by. In my mind, a horse was keeping pace with us, its mane flowing elegantly in the wind, head thrown back, and hooves clopping along the asphalt. When that got too boring, the horse became a giant T-Rex, thick scaly legs pounding against the ground with talons scraping the road, but as exciting as a T-Rex was, I knew it wasn't real. Every ten-year-old on the planet knew that a dinosaur could easily outrun a car, even the NASCAR cars.

If this was a life-or-death situation, my mother and I would be gobbled up in a second by any sort of T-Rex. Sure, my developing karate skills were useful, but they didn't exactly protect against apex predators.

"Why the long face?" Mom asked, glancing at me in the mirror. She arched a brow expectantly as I slowly adjusted my posture.

"I don't know, I'm just bored I guess," I shrugged, letting my head settle against the window once more. The vibrations of the car made my brain go fuzzy and the inner part of my ears itch.

"Do you want me to put on that podcast you like?" She offered, giving me an encouraging smile. I didn't have the heart to tell her that I didn't *actually* like the podcast. I only said I did because I knew it made her happy.

"Sure, you can play it," I nodded, knowing full well that she was already switching off the radio and connecting her phone to the car speakers. Without much of a warning, a deep male voice filled the silence of the car with over pronounced words and too much attempted charisma. Overall, it was too fake for my liking, and the absurdity was almost enough to ease me to sleep. If it wasn't for the way my head bounced lightly against the car window, I would have been out like a light.

Perhaps that would have been better looking back on it.

At some point during the extensive drive, something caught my eye for only a second amongst the dense tree line. It was a flash of human skin. As if someone were standing there waiting to be picked up by a long-haul trucker. I'd heard about hitch hikers, but I'd never seen one. It was common knowledge nowadays that hitch hiking was dangerous. Let alone in the middle of nowhere by a highway bordering the woods.

Frowning, I tried to look back at the weird individual, but they were long gone. Pursing my lips I settled back in my seat, my interest waning once more when tan colored skin reflected in the rear-view mirror. Confused, I peered out the window to find some odd creature loping along beside us. It looked like the horse I'd imagined earlier, long hair flapping in the wind, muzzle snorting heavily with each breath.

The chances of such a thing happening had to be astronomically low, but here I was witnessing one of the greatest events in my life. Awe took over any sort of logic as I smashed my face into the glass and my hands plastered themselves to the window. My excited breath created a foggy haze against the   cool windowpane disguising the horse as it kept pace.

If it wasn't crazy enough that a horse was chasing my car down the highway, the fact that it was following us unbothered was even crazier. Giddy and wide awake, I waited impatiently to make it home. If I got lucky the horse would follow us all the way back. Keeping my eyes on the flash of color beside me, I only looked away to glance at the clock.

At some point the neighborhood came into view with a plethora of glittering lights. As the car started to slow, the horse began to trot even slower. So much so that it disappeared. To say I was disappointed would be an understatement. With a heavy sigh I resigned myself to the fact that having a horse follow me home was too good to be true.

Trying not to let on that anything particularly interesting had happened on the car ride home, I followed Mom's lead as she unbuckled her seat belt. Having parked in the driveway, I let mom worry about carrying my things inside. My priorities lay elsewhere. Standing at the end of the driveway I tried to find the horse. Part of me expected to see it loping along the neighborhood street but there was nothing.

It occurred to me that maybe in my tiredness I'd made it all up. Or at the very least I'd fallen asleep, and Mom had woken me up from a dream. Those were the only explanations I could think of as to why a mighty stallion wasn't snuffling around the empty street.

"Come on Julian. Dad and Will made dinner!" Mom called, making her way back outside and gesturing for me to follow her. Bowing my head, I ventured into the house where life returned to normal. Dad told us about his day at work moving forklifts and heavy materials. My older brother Will made a point of mocking me for my karate uniform and my measly orange belt. Most of the time I let things slide, but tonight I was particularly agitated.

"Do you always have to make fun of me?" I asked, frowning so hard my nose scrunched up.

"It's my job as a big brother. When you get bigger, you'll look less stupid in the uniform," he assured, disguising his insult as an attempted compliment.

Rolling my eyes, I ate what I wanted before retreating to my room. There was only one thing that'd make me feel better after the disappointing lack of a horse and the biting words of my brother: a warm shower. Now that fall was rolling in, the temperature was beginning to drop, which meant that hot showers were the best way to end the night. I could steam up the bathroom creating a cocoon of heat before changing into my pajamas and escaping to my bed. It was the perfect plan.

Pleased with my arrangements, I heard the vague discussion of my parents and Will still at the dinner table. I didn't care too much about what was being said, only that Will was going to chop up some firewood before tomorrow morning's storm rolled in. Truthfully, the only perk about being the younger brother was that all the extra chores went to Will instead of me.

 Humming one of the overplayed songs from the radio, I finished up my shower and successfully snuggled up bed. With my favorite pillow in place accompanied by a careful assortment of stuffed animals, nothing could go wrong. What awaited me was a nice cozy night of pleasant dreams and soft snores. At least, that was the plan after I finished up my book. Waiting patiently for both Mom and Dad to bid me goodnight I tucked Jeremy Joules and the Space Ghouls alongside a flashlight underneath my covers. At long last, Mom and Dad made an appearance, kissed me good night, and when I was certain they were gone, I took to reading beneath my covers.

Smiling smugly to myself for successfully fooling my parents, I set to work on finishing the last 50 pages. As I read, I could hear the distinct sound of my brother hacking away at a series of logs. To say I got satisfaction at the idea of him freezing his butt off while I got to read Jeremy Joules and the Space Ghouls snuggled up in bed would be an understatement.

Grinning like an idiot, I held the flashlight aloft, absorbed in the story when the sound of an arching axe ceased. I assumed that Will had finished his chore for the night and was bound to head inside at any moment. If he caught me hiding out under my covers past my bedtime, he'd surely snitch. After all, that's what older brothers did.

Shutting off the flashlight and marking my place, I rolled onto my side faking sleep. I wasn't too good at faking my way through anything in life, but I'd mastered the art of false slumber. It was almost necessary in order to read past my bedtime.

Waiting impatiently for the sound of Will's shower starting up, I became incredibly anxious when the sound of rushing water never came. The house was only this quiet when Will was plotting something. For a moment I imagined him planning an elaborate trap to ruin my morning. He could be rifling through the fridge creating an evil concoction. He'd inevitably put it in the hot sauce bottle knowing I liked hot sauce on my eggs in the morning. The thought alone made my stomach churn.

Under normal circumstances I wouldn't bother thwarting my brother's plans, but when the house was *still* dead silent, a cautious bravery came over me. Flicking on my flashlight, I slid out of bed, stepped into my fluffy red slippers, and ventured out into the hallway. Looking left and right as if I were crossing a road, I made a sharp turn towards the kitchen. Padding softly across the floor I expected to see my brother at any moment. Hell, I wouldn't even care if I found him drinking straight out of the milk carton so long as he was alive.

Holding my breath, I tip-toed towards the kitchen, rounded the corner, and there he was chugging orange juice like his life depended on it. Letting out a sigh of relief, I couldn't help but hug him. He was so surprised by the gesture he nearly choked on his juice. Screwing the cap back on the bottle, he hesitantly patted me on the head.

"I thought you died," I worried, taking a step back to look at him. His cheeks were flushed red from the cold and the effort of chopping wood.

"Why would I be dead?" He asked, confusion painting his face.

"I don't know, I just didn't hear you come inside. I thought you disappeared or something," I admitted, offering up a shrug.

"Well, I'm not dead or disappeared so chill out," Will insisted. "I just came in late. Thought I heard some sort of dog by the wood pile."

"Was there?" I asked, turning to look at the front door.

"Nah," Will replied, shaking his head.

"Are you sure? What if it's just scared and hiding? It could be a little one." The thought of a puppy nestled into the crevices of the wood pile broke my heart. It would be freezing and likely starving or even scared.

"Okay, okay, before you start crying, I'll go back outside and check again. Just go back to bed and don't bother me again," Will frowned, setting the orange juice back in the fridge. As he closed the refrigerator door and made his way out of the kitchen, a wave of unfounded anxiety washed over me.

Taking a few hasty breaths, I convinced myself to go back to bed. Will would be safe outside by himself. He even knew how to use the axe. If shit really hit the fan, he could defend himself with it. Of course, if Will was just trying to find a lost puppy there was nothing to be worried about. Shaking my head, I chalked up my worries to an overactive imagination. We lived in a close-knit neighborhood. Bad things didn't happen to people like us.

Keeping my cool, I returned to bed, rolled onto my side, and closed my eyes. Outside I could hear Will walking around, calling out on occasion, and even whistling for the lost puppy. Certain that he'd be okay, my heart rate finally slowed, and at long last I felt tiredness creep into my bones. Half asleep with Jeremy Joules and the Space Ghouls on my mind, I almost missed the sound of tapping on my bedroom window. Blinking sleep from my eyes, I crawled out of bed yet again, and pulled aside my curtains.

Will stood there impatiently with a look of frustration on his face. Rushing to unlatch the window, I noticed that he held a weird looking collar in his hand. Sliding the glass pane up, I peered outside hoping to see a dog.

"You were right, someone dumped a dog around here. I found the collar," Will explained. "I keep getting close, but the poor thing runs away every time."

"Maybe if you get some food, you can lure it out? I can come help if you want. I could even get Mom and Dad!"

"No, you'll only get in the way. The dog keeps heading off into the woods by the house. Besides, Mom and Dad are *not* gonna trek all the way out there for a stray dog," Will insisted. Holding out the collar he gave me an expectant look. "Just hang onto this for now. Once I get the little guy, we can put it back on him."

"Okay." Nodding, I took the collar and held it close to my chest. "Be careful, the woods aren't safe at night. There could be bobcats."

"I'll be fine. I'm not a big ole sissy like you. Just hang tight. And don't say I never did anything for you," Will smirked, turning curtly on his heel and jogging off towards the side of the house. Easing the window shut, I let my curtains fall back into place and settled the dog collar on my nightstand.

This time, instead of getting back in bed, I waited impatiently at my desk. Leg bouncing up and down I said a silent prayer for Will's safe return. For all either of us knew, the woods by our house contained bears, coyotes, or even serial killers. As time continued to pass, I grew even more anxious until another knock sounded at my window. Immediately, and without thinking, I tossed open my curtains and threw open my window.

What waited for me on the other side wasn't Will. It was a familiar tan looking creature with long stringy hair. It stood on two legs, long and wiry, with angled ankles like that of a dog. Its torso was impossibly human. The creature was emaciated, with skin stretched taught over bones so that when it breathed, I could see each individual rib. A set of arms stuck out of its rib cage about six inches down from its other set of arms. The ones growing from its torso were skinny but strong, with large, calloused hands and pointy claws. The second set of arms were twice as long, originating at the shoulders as all arms should. The creature's fingers were impossibly long, dangling uselessly at its side. But the most horrifying part of the monster was its face. It had a long horse like snout, full of canine teeth dripping and oozing with saliva. Its mouth was so crowded a perpetual smile rested on its face. Long stringy hair ran from its head down along its spine. Its eyes were narrow and placed close together.

Staring wide eyed at the creature, I watched as its lanky arms continued to tap at my window frame as if it hadn't realized I'd already opened my window. Taking a step back, I nearly tripped and fell into my bed. Heart hammering, I glanced from the window to my bedroom door and back again. The monster remained in place for quite some time, breathing heavily, horse-like nostrils flaring. A firm breeze wafted through the window and the creature's pupils dilated. Its gaze shifted to the collar settled on my nightstand.

Its teeth chattered eerily, slobber dripping onto the floorboards as it leaned forward through the window. Its incredibly long upper arm snaked along the wall, nails scraping over the stucco, fumbling towards the collar. Grabbing the collar, the monster's arms shot back out of the window as if it'd been electrocuted. Sniffing hungrily at the collar, the creature unclasped the red piece of leather and beckoned me forward.

Throat dry, I took a step back sitting firmly on my bed. Picking my feet up off the floor as if that would help protect me, I refused to take my eyes off the horrifying monster in front of me. Its teeth began to chatter in response to my actions, it's growing irritation causing slobber to patter onto the floor in a pool. Its frustration mounted into an inhuman type of grunting, tantrum like flailing of the collar, and loud snuffling. Panicking, I realized that if the monster's distress grew there was no telling what it'd do.

Standing I held out my hands to placate it. Almost immediately the creature's rage subsided. It passed over the collar and settled awkwardly onto its haunches like an overgrown dog. Rotating so that its back faced me, the beast remained rigid and still. It occurred to me then that whatever this thing was, it belonged to someone and wanted its collar back on. I wasn't sure who would keep such a monstrosity for a pet, but I got the impression that just like a dog, this ugly creature liked to chase cars.

"You followed me home from karate, didn't you?" I asked, cringing as I brushed the beast's oily hair aside. It was so thin it felt like a bunch of baby spider legs running over my hands. Biting back a gag, I slipped the collar around its neck and fastened it in the back. As soon as the sound of the buckle reached the monster's ear, it spun about excitedly, stood back up to its towering height and licked me. Its long meaty tongue left a streak of thick slobbery mucus along my cheek.

"Ew." Pulling back, I went to wipe away the nasty spittle from my cheek when I noticed the monster's saddened expression. "I mean, thanks."

Spinning in a circle and snuffling, the monster took off down the road, its lower set of arms snapping not action as it bounded along like a horse. Staring out the window as cold air continued to seep into my room, I was startled by Will who appeared in the space the monster had left behind.

"No dog," Will sighed, shaking his head. "I walked all over the place back there and saw nothing. Whatever it was it's gone now so go to sleep."

"Yeah, yeah I will," I nodded.

"You look like you've seen a ghost," Will frowned,

"Something like that," I muttered, sliding my window down and closing the curtains.

For the final time that night I clambered into bed, but instead of thinking about Jeremey Joules and the Space Ghouls, I thought about the weird monster. Without a doubt, I was certain that it was the strange horse that'd run alongside the car. While I didn't know where it came from, I was glad it'd turned out to be friendly. But what scared me more was not knowing who the window runner belonged to. What kind of person kept something that hideous and big? Were they mean? Did they eat little kids?

No matter how hard I tried I couldn't stop thinking about it. If creatures like that existed, why hadn't anyone reported them? Why didn't anyone have pictures of them? Why didn't anyone talk about them?

As I continued to spiral in thought I came to a particularly terrifying conclusion. The only reason monsters like that weren't seen is because they weren't supposed to be. And if they were seen, no one lived to tell of it. Which meant one of two things:

1. I'd gotten extremely lucky.

2. The monster had done exactly what it was supposed to. It'd followed me, tracked me, watched me, gotten my scent, tasted my flesh, and made sure I bore witness to its existence. And then, in my childish naivety, I sent it home with a fresh target; **me**.

Lakeside

I never expected to see Evelyn by the lake. Not after so much time apart. She stopped coming around a few months ago much to my surprise. It hurt my feelings at first, but I came to terms with the fact that she was simply growing, changing, becoming an adult. I was a few years behind her, which meant life's responsibilities hadn't claimed me yet.

I watched as she glanced from side to side as if she were afraid of being spotted before sliding down the sandy hillside of Lake Tombstone. Her beautiful blonde hair was braided as usual and tied about her head in an elegant crown. Her pale skin was likely coated with a thin layer of sunscreen. She had a habit of getting burned. I used to scold her about it back when we lived in the same neighborhood.

As she made her way across the soft sand, I found that the sound of her footsteps soothed me. The pattern of her stride was something I'd come to recognize long ago. The way her heels always seemed to drag a millisecond too long with each step. Or the way she had a slightly louder footfall when stepping with her right leg instead of her left.

As I took in the comfort of her presence a breeze carried the smell of Lake Tombstone across the sandy shore and through its nearby weeds. It consisted of mud, musty water, crisp trees, and pollen. It used to smell much different, cleaner, fresher, but the weeds had grown since the last time Evelyn visited. It all came down to the fact that people didn't come here anymore. The lake wasn't taken care of the way it used to be, which meant its murky ugly water scared people off. Because of this fishermen and vacation goers stayed clear of the area opting for cleaner more appealing environments full of life and flowers.

While I could understand their apprehension, I didn't mind. I liked the wild nature of the lake. It wasn't meant to be domesticated. The wilder the better. Too many places were being industrialized nowadays and frankly I didn't want to put up with the horrible sound of excavators.

"Hello, Josephine." Evelyn's voice interrupted my thoughts with its light and airy lilt. She never had much weight to her tone, but her words always carried a hint of despair. Even when we were little, she seemed to have an unseen burden in her language. Like she knew one day she'd experience a tragedy most people wouldn't understand. It used to amuse me. Now it made me sad.

"Hi," I smiled, watching as she stretched out a beach towel. She seemed hesitant about being here. Skittish even. With a small shake of the head, she took her place beside me in the sand. She slid off her brown leather sandals and adjusted the skirt of her summer dress before crossing her legs. She was more of a beautiful woman than I would ever be.

"How have you been?" Evelyn asked, tucking a loose trans of blonde hair behind her ear. "It's been a long time since I've been here."

"It has. I thought you wouldn't come back," I laughed, trying not to sound grim or down trod. As much as her absence pained me, I was elated to see her again. This was our spot. The spot Evelyn and I used to talk about our darkest secrets. The spot where we had double dates when we were still too young to date. The spot where we left adolescence behind and grew into teenagers. "But to answer your question, not much has changed. It's the usual for me."

"I see," Evelyn nodded, pursing her lips in thought before letting out a heavy sigh. "Josephine, you know I can't come around the way I used to, don't you?"

"Of course!" Nodding, I picked up a smooth rock and skipped it across the surface of the lake. The ripples were so small they didn't seem to exist. It was almost like the rock was weightless, floating instead of falling.

"I have a family now," Evelyn continued. "Responsibilities that I didn't used to have. It takes more time and energy than I would have thought. I guess I should've listened to you about having kids. They are exhausting."

"They are, but you always yearned for the domestic life. You never liked the adventures I had you go on. Just hang in there. Every change in life is an adjustment. You'll get used to it you just have to give yourself some time," I encouraged, watching as she pulled a frayed string from the old beach towel. She was nervous. As her brow furrowed in thought I almost dreaded what she'd say next.

"My little boy," Evelyn began, a tentative smile making its way onto her face, "I named him after you. His name is Joseph, but I like to call him Joey. It's fitting considering I used to think your name was Joey."

"You can blame that on my parents," I laughed, feeling my chest tighten with a strange melancholy feeling. "He must be a great kid. Hopefully he takes after you."

Silence settled between us for longer than I would have liked. In truth I wasn't sure what to say to break the tension, but I also knew that Evelyn was avoiding conversation. She wasn't here for small talk. She was here for something more troubling. Something she didn't want to talk about.

"Josephine, I know I said that I'd look out for you. I promised a long time ago that I would, but I don't know if I can anymore. No matter how hard I try, I'm just not good enough," Evelyn sighed, bowing her head in the dimming light. She seemed to withdraw into herself like she was trying to hide. As she sat quietly I turned my attention to the sky where the sun was beginning to set. As the sun began to sink goodnight it painted the sky in a plethora of reds.

"You'll always be good enough for me," I assured, settling my hand on top of hers. "And for the record, you did protect me. I got myself into trouble, not you. It's not your fault that-
"

"I just get overwhelmed, and I can't help but wonder how many are out there in the water," Evelyn muttered, brow furrowed.

"How many what?" I asked, taken aback by her interruption.

"How many bodies," Evelyn continued her voice whispery in nature. "When you really think about it, how many bodies are out there in the ocean, in the rivers, in the lakes? It's got to be a lot, right?"

"I would suppose so," I nodded, trying not to think too much about that fact.

"And yet, out of all the places they've searched, out of all the rivers and lakes, none of them...none of them…" Evelyn shivered, sniffling ever so slightly as if she were fighting back tears unable to finish her sentence.

"Well, there's always more places to search, right?" Nudging her with my elbow, I turned my attention back to the blood-colored sky. It'd be dark soon and she'd have to go.

"More? How many more? They've covered every waterway in this damn town," Evelyn argued, hugging herself tightly. Her blue eyes welled with tears and her bottom lip trembled. "How am I ever going to find you?"

"You will," I promised, hoping she'd feel optimistic the way she used to. "You will find me. You'll know it when you do."

"And if I don't?" Evelyn whispered, wiping her eyes with shaking hands.

"Then I guess you'll just have to keep looking," I shrugged. "Lake Tombstone isn't going to be here forever. Not with how much it's dried up and grown weeds. Give it time."

"I don't know if I can do this anymore," Evelyn sobbed, her head falling into her hands. "Nothing I do is working, nothing I say is taken seriously, and nobody believes me that you're dead. You're just gone Josephine. That's all anyone knows for sure."

"Then make them listen to you! Make them hear what you have to say, please Evelyn- "

"It doesn't help that the cops don't care. To them you're just a poor small-town girl that vanished. They think you went away for a better life. Like you're some idiotic teenager running off with a long-haul trucker or something. How am I supposed to argue with that?" Evelyn worried, spiraling with each vocalized thought.

"Find me, Evelyn."

"Who am I kidding? I can't even call it arguing; I don't have evidence. They say my gut instinct isn't enough proof but how am I supposed to get proof if they won't let me look anywhere?" Evelyn growled, anger taking over her sorrows as the moon began to crawl its way into the sky. The clouds shrouded it from reality smothering the only thing I looked forward to at this time of night. Then, at last, the moon forced its way through sending a silvery light over Lake Tombstone.

"Evelyn, you promised you'd find me."

"I promised, I know," Evelyn nodded. "I know what I promised."

With a shaky sigh, she struggled to her feet, collected the beach towel, gave it a firm shake, and turned to leave. She didn't take more than two steps before turning back towards the water.

"I will find you, Josephine. I know you're out there. "Somewhere, anyways," Evelyn insisted, jaw set in determination. "Just, don't go anywhere."

"Wasn't planning on it," I laughed, standing alone on the lakeside shivering from head to toe as the water grew cold. With a definitive nod, Evelyn made her way back across the sandy terrain and disappeared.

Bowing my head, I turned towards the water. Stepping into it hesitantly the lake's bitter touch sent a shock through me. As quickly as it came it passed just as fast. Holding my breath, I pressed on until the top of my head dipped below the surface of the lake. Blinking through the dark murky water, I took the familiar path back home.

Weaving through a set of weeds and long grass, I came across a pile of large misshapen rocks. Rocks that I'd become accustomed to. They were fused together like a strange tumor, not exactly smooth but not dangerously sharp. Beside them lay the body of a girl, long decomposed with decaying skin floating lazily in the water. It reminded me of potato peels only these were much worse. The girl's eyes had sunk back into her head leaving shallow holes behind. In one of them an old fishing hook had made its bed. Then there was her hair. It'd withered, stiffened, until tiny fish used it for cover. Around her ankles were chains and along with the chains there were stones. Smooth stones, not strange like the rest of the rocks.

Pinned to the lake floor and unable to make her way to the surface even if she wanted to, the girl had become a fixture to the surrounding area. She'd become a statue for local wildlife to gawk at and leave behind. In truth, she was a beautifully tragic sight, one that was difficult to acknowledge by anyone other than the fish.

With a soft sigh, I settled into place, fixing the shackles around my ankles, feeling the weight of the stones against my body, and the fish tickle my scalp all while the moon watched over me. Anyone else would be oblivious to where I lay against the silt covered floor. Anyone else would stay at the lakeside and be safe. Anyone else would have refused to go on a boat ride with people she thought were her friends. Anyone else would have known that amongst all the waterways in the world, only the one named Lake Tombstone would hold true to its name. Anyone else would still be alive.

But not Josephine. Not me. I wasn't anyone else. I was dead. No one was going to find me. Not even Evelyn.

The Mountain

She used to believe in God the way most innocent children do. It's hard to deny the words of your parents and it's even harder to not believe in something good. She didn't know any better. No one really does. Not until they come to terms with who they really believe in.

That was the case for naive little Ellie. She packed her bags eagerly under the supervision of her father, finally old enough to partake in a family tradition. According to her father it began at the start of their family lineage. As far as Ellie was concerned, that was a very long time.

"Make sure you have your bear spray," Dad warned, shoving a sleeping bag into the confines of his pack.

"Are there really bears up there, Daddy?" Ellie asked, turning the pressurized can over in her hands. She'd heard stories of bears, mountain lions, and bob cats running across the wilderness untamed. More concerning was the fact that the animals of The Mountain had claimed a fair share of her relatives.

Uncle Jeremy was mauled to death at 12 years of age. Then there was great great uncle Clyde who was eaten alive by a bobcat over the course of three days. Of course, there was great great great great uncle Cletus who was killed by an Elk in a freak accident. Perhaps the most infamous death was that of her fourth removed cousin Susan being swept up by a large eagle at the age of six and plucked into pieces.

"There's all sorts of things up there," Dad answered, guiding her small hands away from the bear spray and clipping it to his belt.

"What if the bears chase us?" Ellie worried, holding her arms out expectantly as Dad placed the backpack on her shoulders.

"We just make a lot of noise, and the bears won't bother us."

"What about the elk? What if they get after us like they did Cletus?"

"They won't."

"Are you sure?"

"Positive," Dad sighed, framing her face in his hands. "Those were just freak accidents. Besides, I've prayed for safe passage every night for the past week. It's a family tradition. A coming-of-age ceremony. We go to the top, pray, camp there overnight, fast, and return home."

"Do we really have to fast?" Ellie groaned, imagining what it'd be like to hike down The Mountain on an empty stomach.

"It's tradition. Now, go kiss your mother goodbye we need to get going before it's too late," Dad urged, preparing the last of his supplies as Ellie went to find her mother.

As the youngster expected, her mother was walking amongst the fields of their homestead fending off birds and other predators. A murder of crows took flight in a flurry of wings as Ellie approached hugging her mother tightly beneath the warm sun.

They said a quick prayer together asking for safe passage before kissing each other goodbye. Ellie ran to the fence line where her father stood waiting, back burdened by large bundles of supplies. He looked strong to her, as most fathers do to their little girls. He was an indomitable man with the spirit and drive to carry her through any troubles.

Together, both father and daughter waved goodbye to the woman in the fields and set off towards their trail of tradition, Ellie holding her father's hand.

Their trek started out simple enough, a plain gravel path leading them in the right direction. Not a single rock was out of place as if it were tended to quite regularly. As the path wove its way back into the countryside along the base of The Mountain, Ellie pulled away from her father. The call of adventure much stronger than the call of safety.

Venturing into the tree line, young Ellie gawked at steadfast wooden warriors, their green covered limbs stretching out across the sky. Large birds flew in and out of sight, wings beating the air into submission as if they were angels of the sky. Sure, she was used to nature in all its wild glory, but not like this. There was something different about The Mountain.

"You know to stay on the trail, yes?" Dad called, drawing Ellie's attention.

"Of course!" Ellie nodded, circling back to her dad. Like before she nestled her small hand in his calloused palm. His large fingers wrapped around her wrist entirely and together they moved on.

As the trail grew steeper, Ellie grew tired, the weight of her pack making it more difficult than before to keep up with the long strides of her father. Determined, she did her best not to show her struggles, silently praying that God would give her super strength. Of course, that's not how God works and instead of a divine being coming to her aid, it was her earthly father.

"Here." Offering up a supportive smile, Ellie's father took her pack and carried it in hand unburdened by the weight. Unlike his daughter he was stronger than an ox, growing up wild and free alongside his brothers. The homestead had made its way into his hands as he was the eldest. Because of this, it was his responsibility to honor tradition, which meant raising timid daughters subjected to the will of man.

"Daddy?" Ellie questioned, huffing and puffing along. "How much longer until bedtime?"

"Just a few more hours. Why don't we take a break for snacks?" he asked, sensing his daughter's growing distress.

"I like that idea," Ellie grinned, plopping down in the middle of the trail, and crossing her legs.

As they ate, Ellie pressed her father about the tragedies that riddled The Mountain. Her curiosity was something her father couldn't curb regardless of the topic. He was hesitant to fill his daughter's head with stories of bear attacks and elk accidents, but she was persistent.

"Cletus was walking up this very path when he spooked a giant Elk. Normally they don't attack, but this Elk was different. For some reason it had murder on its mind. Cletus didn't stand a chance. Those antlers can snap you up like a twig," he explained, wrapping up the other half of his sandwich.

"Was it possessed or something?" Ellie asked, nibbling at the remaining crust of her PB&J.

"Not possessed. No, the Devil was working in that creature. God's got a strong presence here. He always has, but where there's God there's the Devil too."

"How do you know it was the Devil? What if God just didn't like Cletus?" Ellie mused, slowly getting to her feet refreshed and ready to walk.

"God talks to people. The Devil doesn't. God tells us what we need to do, and the Devil does what he can to prevent that.

God told Cletus to go up the mountain. The Devil killed Cletus before he could get there," Dad explained, joining Ellie on the path once more. While it seemed like an existential explanation, Ellie didn't ask any other questions. To her it made sense. The Devil was a snake after all, and snakes couldn't talk.

As day turned to night, the duo huddled close together in a small tent, Ellie tucked into her father's side. Snuggled up in a sleeping bag she fell asleep listening to the sound of grasshoppers and their violin songs. In truth she never felt safer than when she was held by her Dad. There was just something about his arms holding her tight that made all the bad things in the world go away, including bears.

The morning progressed with a warm bowl of oatmeal, cuddles, and reassurances that the rest of the journey would be just as easy as the first day. Ellie believed her father as most children do, and together they continued their journey uninterrupted. It wasn't until the third day that things began to change. Not for Ellie, but for her father.

As the air grew thinner and exhaustion crept into his bones, he began to hear the nagging voice of God. A God he prayed to each night along with his daughter, only this time it wasn't such an innocent discussion.

"You know what you must do, my child," God directed, voice soft and inviting.

"I don't," Dad replied, watching Ellie clamber over a tree that'd fallen across the path.

"You do. It's tradition," God encouraged. *"You know what becomes of those on this mountain. Your will is not exercised here. It is mine that you must follow."*

Shaking his head, Dad tried to carry on, but there was the feeling that something ominous was watching him. A set of eyes all seeing and inescapable watched him from a place he could not see. He was not safe here, but could he really run from God? Wasn't he a faithful man to his Heavenly Father?

"What's wrong, Daddy?" Ellie asked, appearing before her father with the concerned face only a child could have. Her eyes were tender, sweet, earnest.

"Nothing, sweetie. Daddy is just thinking, that's all," he insisted, adjusting her backpack so it sat properly on her shoulders. "I'm just a little tired and when I get tired, I get quiet."

Taking the answer at face value, Ellie didn't bother her father again. Not until she lay beside him in the sleeping bag, aware of his whispered prayers. He rambled extensively, much longer than normal, and while it was a little unnerving Ellie figured he was having an important discussion with God. Sort of like the time she asked God to give her a baby brother. She'd spent an hour begging and pleading with her Heavenly Father to no avail.

As for Ellie's father, he slept restlessly talking in his sleep to God and the grasshoppers. Even when morning came, he was talking. Talking to himself, pausing only to address Ellie, then talking to God, and finally himself again.

"What will you do when you get there?" God asked, voice patronizing in nature. *"Are you to turn from me my faithful servant? After all I have done for you, would you disgrace me?"*

"Of course not," Dad argued, eyes trained on the trail. It was growing harder and harder to breathe let alone think. The Mountain had grown progressively steeper with each step and soon he'd need to crawl on all fours just to keep from tumbling backwards. As for Ellie, she made light work of the hike weighing a fraction of her father. Gravity was kind to her.

"I see doubt in your heart, child."

"There's no doubt, just….consideration."

"You don't trust me?"

"No, I trust you it's just…difficult. I never thought I'd be asked to do this. I've only ever read about it. I assumed I'd never face the same consequence." Dad breathed, clawing his way through the dirt. Jamming his knees into the ground he carried on, struggling to breathe with each second that passed. How high had they gone? Was the air getting thinner? Had it always been this hard to breathe? Grunting, Dad moved on, nails biting into soil.

All around the trees watched him grovel along the path like a worm. He was nothing. Just a creature created to serve a man he didn't truly understand or know.

"Daddy!" Ellie cried, gravel raining down on her father's head as she began to slide backwards. As her backpack sent her toppling down, her father snapped out of his stupor long enough to catch her. Grasped at the heel and dangling like a worm on a hook, Ellie's backpack slipped free and carried on down the hill.

"I've got you baby girl," he breathed. "Hold on."

Bracing himself against the mountainside, Dad pulled his daughter into a tight embrace, the smell of sweat and dirt permeating the air between them. Letting out a heavy sigh, he shed the largest of his two packs and slung Ellie across his shoulders.

"Are you sure we should keep going? It's so steep," Ellie worried, bottom lip trembling as her adrenaline began to crash.

"We have to. It's tradition," Dad reminded, pressing his forehead into the dirt. Collecting himself, he carried on, fighting his way forward with lunging strides.

For a while the voice of God stopped as he focused on the task at hand, but the higher they climbed the louder it became. With God's blessing and encouragement, Dad became stronger than anything Ellie had ever seen before. He clambered up the side of the mountain to crest the top at long last. Collapsing in a heap, delirious from effort, Dad struggled to catch his breath as Ellie showered him in kisses.

"You did it Daddy! That was incredible!" Ellie exclaimed, using the hem of her shirt to wipe the dirt from his face. In his stupor, he began to ramble once more. God was close, so near it sent shivers down his spine.

"Well done my son."

"Let me rest. Let me pray," Dad begged.

"You have work to do. Your faith has brought you here. Don't let it dwindle alongside your strength. Rise. Do as I have asked."

"I just need a minute," Dad growled, eyes screwed shut as if he were in pain.

"What are you talking about, Daddy?" Ellie frowned, sitting back on her heels. "Are you tired? I can set up the tent the way you showed me. Then we can pray, stay the night, fast, and go home! Mom's gonna be waiting for us."

"Trust in me child," God whispered, voice traveling through the wind. *"Believe in me."*

With a heavy sigh, and teary eyes, Dad moved from where he lay. Staggering to his feet he turned towards Ellie and held out his hand. Without hesitation she took it and together they made their way towards the center of the mountain top.

Half dragging, half pulling her father, Ellie paused at the sight before her. In the center of the mountain peak was a slab of stone cut from the ground around it. Like an altar, the stone was unblemished, unnaturally so, its surface a rusty red across the top. Scattered around the base of the altar were bones of varying sizes and colors. Some had been charred, others snapped into pieces, and some whole. Stomach churning, Ellie looked to her father for an answer. Why did such a desolate area have so many corpses?

"Animal bones," Dad assured, smoothing out her hair. "Let's set up the tent."

Nodding, Ellie obeyed. Rummaging through her father's backpack she pulled free the stakes for the tent. Setting things in their respective place she waited impatiently for her father to hoist up the canvas structure.

At long last the tent stood erect, the only other landmark that claimed the mountaintop as its own. Seeking refuge in its small confines, Ellie pulled free her Bible flicking rapidly through the pages searching for a prayer to ease her worries. Something wasn't sitting right with her, but she couldn't place it. It wasn't until her father gently took the book away and held her that she relaxed.

"We made it," Dad smiled thinly, though sweat still clung to his features. "Let's get started, shall we?"

"We pray first, right?" Ellie asked.

"Yes," he nodded, sitting idly by as Ellie bowed her head. Taking a deep breath, she poured her heart out on top of The Mountain.

"Dear Heavenly Father, it's me, Ellie. I know you're probably really busy, but I just made it to the top of The Mountain with my dad. It was crazy scary, but he took good care of me. He says we have to pray now so that's what I'm doing," Ellie giggled, smiling to herself. "I want to say thank you for giving me such a wonderful Daddy. I want to say thank you for my Mommy too, and if you can I'd love to have a little brother. Other than that, I ask that you keep Daddy and I safe from all the bears up here. I ask that you help us feel your presence and grow our faith in the time we have together. I've never been this close to heaven before, so I hope that helps you hear me."

As Ellie continued to pray, Dad watched her, took note of the smile on her face, the innocence in her features, the paleness of her skin, and the lamb-like nature of her youth. Swallowing tightly, he regarded his daughter in a different light than he had before. Her faith was so strong, so pure. She didn't ask questions. She didn't contest God's will. She was graceful in all things including her curiosity.

"The faith of a child will always be stronger than that of an adult," God sighed, his whispered tone pulsing in the air. *"She doesn't ask questions the way you do."*

"She has nothing to lose," Dad countered, hands trembling.

"She has everything to lose, my son, and so do you should you fail my task," he reminded. *"You did not come here to save her. You came here to save yourself."*

"No, I came here for tradition," Dad argued, pulse reeling as he began to see red.

"And tradition demands you follow course as your ancestors have."

"What will it take for you to leave me alone? After all the years I spent talking to you, now you talk back? In what universe does a Heavenly Father ignore his child?"

"In a universe where his faith isn't true. Prove it, and we will speak freely for eternity. Your soul unblemished by doubt and your faith renewed. Don't forget I see the intricacies of your heart. Your loyalty has been tainted for years like that of your brother's." God glowered, words harsh despite their gentle nature.

Shaking his head, Dad clenched his jaw, heart hammering in a painful series of palpitations. All the while he could hear the small words of his daughter speaking to a God she didn't know.

"And Jesus I want to say thank you for your sacrifice. One day when I see you, I'll kiss your hands better," Ellie continued, unaware of her father getting to his feet. In determined movements, he snatched up a coil of rope, lashed it about her wrists, and knotted it so tightly she yelped in pain.

Eyes snapping open she regarded her father in surprise and confusion.

"Daddy?"

Unconcerned, Dad continued his ministrations, forcing his daughter onto her back and lashing up her ankles. Strewn up like cattle, Ellie was hoisted into the air and slung over her father's shoulders. For the first time in her life, she was afraid to be in her father's arms.

"Daddy what are you doing? What's happening?" She cried, panic setting in as he moved towards the altar. "Daddy! Daddy stop!"

"It's okay, Ellie," Dad grunted, setting her across the cold surface of a blood-soaked stone. "You'll be alright. It's just like the Bible. God will protect you."

"What do you mean?" Ellie worried, eyes wide as she squirmed in her restraints. "Daddy, what do you mean?"

"See it through, son. As Abraham did to Isaac," God encouraged, a hand settling on the shoulder of a man who would not defy his God.

"Like Abraham to Isaac," Dad repeated, beads of sweat running down the back of his neck.

"No, Daddy, no!" Ellie cried out, realization setting in. She knew the story of Abraham and Isaac. A story that had always been told to her as harmless was now a terrifying reality.

"It's okay, sweetie. God will save us. Both of us. Have faith," Dad breathed, smoothing her hair down as he rummaged in his pocket. Pulling free a large pocketknife he regarded his daughter once more. "He'll take care of you. Like Abraham and Isaac."

With the sound of crying and screaming as an accompaniment Dad held the blade aloft, eyes closed, and plunged it towards the chest of his little girl. The blade hit with a loud thud, metal scraping through bone before the tip rammed into the stone beneath Ellie's body.

Heaving breaths wracked the man's body. God had gone quiet. His only friend was the breeze. With hesitation he peeled his eyes open to see his hands clutching the hilt of a knife that lay buried in his daughter's chest. Disbelief was the first to manifest followed by betrayal.

"No, no, no," he stammered, staggering back with the blade in hand. "No! You lied! You lied to me."

"I did not lie!" God bellowed. *"Like Abraham and Isaac, I tested your faith. I did not promise to spare her."*

"That's the point of the story. You saved him now, save her!" The man cried out.

"The point of the story is to remind you that faith has a cost, and I expect the cost to be paid." God frowned. *"Being saved isn't free, son. I did not save my own child from sacrifice, why should I save yours?"*

Gut churning, twisting, the man turned away from the altar. Turned away from God. With bile in his throat, he ran abandoning his belongings on a whim. Legs carrying him at a speed he could not comprehend, he fell down the steep side of the mountain. Tumbling, turning, his bones cracked and trembled with each somersault.

"You cannot run from me!" God bellowed, voice shaking the trees.

"Yes, I can." The man shuddered, scrambling to his feet and running until he couldn't anymore. He ran until God disappeared on the mountain top alongside his daughter. He ran until the air grew thick and the cloudiness of his mind cleared. He ran despite the gashes on his skin and the brokenness of his bones. He ran until he found his wife exactly as he'd left her.

"What's wrong?" She demanded, running to meet her husband at the gate. "Where's Ellie?"

No sooner had they met each other, the man collapsed, fatigue draining his senses as God's voice became distorted, slow, unnatural.

"God." He panted. "God."

"What happened?"

"God!" He yelled. The sound of God's horrifying noise grated on his nerves until it morphed into the sound of crows flying overhead. In a matter of seconds his head became still, clarity returned, and there was silence in the world around him.

"Honey, you're not making sense." Hands, soft hands framed his face, smoothing over his hair and wiping away stray tears.

God. Where was he? Why wasn't he speaking? Where had he gone? The silence grew painful as his mind churned restlessly, no longer crowded. Thoughtless, voiceless, faithless, the man rose to his feet and staggered inside.

He did not speak, did not eat, did not move for days. He wanted to hear him. Hear God but there was no answer. No semblance of a familiar voice sitting idly by in his mind. He was alone. With hours of emptiness to console him, the man turned to his wife, an understanding in his bones that was better ignored than accepted.

"Ellie," he remarked, voice hoarse.

"Where is she?" His wife asked, trying to be gentle in her anxious worry.

"The bears. They got her," he muttered, his wife's wails falling on deaf ears. The bears had gotten her. That's what had happened. Like it had with Uncle Jeremy. Almost like it had with Uncle Clyde's demise by bobcat or Cletus' death by Elk.

If the man's wife had been any smarter, she would have noticed the can of bear spray at his hip fully intact, unused, unblemished. She would have known that bears don't live in that part of the state. She would have known that Elk accidents don't happen the way Cletus' did. She would have known that The Mountain was a place of death- not worship- but a place of faith, nonetheless.

Which brings a question to mind that many of the faithful choose to avoid:

If God asked you to kill your child, would you do it?

Made in the USA
Monee, IL
08 April 2025

5586bb72-97d0-439f-ba11-3b2de63c8886R01